A smile curve
rendering him ⌷
"My father and ⌷⌷⌷⌷ **one**
small detail in your plan. If I had
never discovered you were alive, it
wouldn't have mattered so much.
But I did."

"What detail?" Ariana was shouting now, her voice lost in the gray bleakness around her. Everything about those few days was still jumbled in her head. She'd been acting on pure animal instincts—fear the overriding one—and listening to King Theos had been the worst kind of mistake.

All she'd wanted was to escape Drakon before Andreas came back from his summit. Before she was caught in the web of her own love for him.

Her leaving him was a betrayal to a man who didn't break rules for anyone, an unforgivable mistake toward a man whose word meant everything.

She clasped his jaw, forcing him to look at her. "What detail, Andreas?"

He still didn't hold her. Didn't touch her in any way. Those eyes trapped her again, until even breathing was a chore. Those eyes betrayed all his emotions—fury, shock and the cold enjoyment of her fate now.

"You are still my wife."

Tara Pammi

HIS DRAKON
RUNAWAY BRIDE

Recycling programs
for this product may
not exist in your area.

ISBN: 978-0-373-06099-3

His Drakon Runaway Bride

First North American publication 2017

Copyright © 2017 by Tara Pammi

Printed in U.S.A.

Tara Pammi can't remember a moment when she wasn't lost in a book—especially a romance, which was much more exciting than a mathematics textbook at school. Years later, Tara's wild imagination and love for the written word revealed what she really wanted to do. Now she pairs alpha males who think they know everything with strong women who knock that theory and them off their feet!

Books by Tara Pammi

Harlequin Presents

The Sheikh's Pregnant Prisoner
The Man to Be Reckoned With
A Deal with Demakis

The Drakon Royals

Crowned for the Drakon Legacy
The Drakon Baby Bargain

Brides for Billionaires

Married for the Sheikh's Duty

The Legendary Conti Brothers

The Surprise Conti Child
The Unwanted Conti Bride

Greek Tycoons Tamed

Claimed for His Duty
Bought for Her Innocence

Society Weddings

The Sicilian's Surprise Wife

A Dynasty of Sand and Scandal

The Last Prince of Dahaar
The True King of Dahaar

Visit the Author Profile page at Harlequin.com for more titles.

CHAPTER ONE

"IS THIS A coup to overthrow me?" Crown Prince Andreas Drakos of Drakon joked as he walked into his study to find his family staring at him with a spectrum of emotions—concern in his sister Eleni's eyes, stubborn resolve in Mia's, something he couldn't define in his brother Nikandros's and pure frost in Gabriel's.

"None of us want your job, your popularity rating or your life, Andreas," replied Nikandros, the financial genius who had set Drakon on its path of recovery after the mess their father had made in the last decade.

Nik was right. The state of his life currently—utter chaos with the Crown Council breathing down his neck for the announcement of his choice for the next Queen of Drakon, the questions the media was raising about his mental health, his frequent disappearances from Drakon in the last year, sometimes even his sexuality—would have usually had the effect of fire ants crawling all over his skin.

But he didn't have any mental energy left beyond the hunt he'd been on for two years now. He was getting close, he knew it in his blood.

He settled down next to Mia. The smell of baby

powder drifting from her was strangely calming. "How are you, Mia?"

Mia took his hands in hers. He tried not to flinch. Physical contact made him twitchy and now Mia knew it. But somewhere in the last few months, his sister-in-law and he had become strangely close.

"You didn't come to see the twins, Andreas. After all the hullabaloo you raised about heirs for Drakon, I'm feeling neglected."

He smiled. "I have just this hour returned to Drakon."

"Which nicely segues to why we are all here. Andreas, what is going on?"

"You let her leave Tia and Alexio's side to ask me this question?" Nik glared at him in response. Dark shadows bruised Mia's eyes. "You look awful."

"Stop posturing, Nik. You know he's just trying to get a rise out of you." She smiled and her eyes lit up with that same incandescent joy he'd seen in Nik's of late. "I have two very good reasons for *my* ghoulish look, Your Highness," she said, her gaze tracing the angles of his face. "You however do not.

"You look like hell," she said with that forthrightness he'd come to expect from her, "and whether Nik and Gabriel will agree to put it like that or not, we're all…very worried about you."

He frowned, looked up and, with a strange knot in his gut, realized it was true. "It's not necessary."

"There's talk from the Crown Council about asking you to step down. Your popularity level is at its lowest," Nik said in a deceptively calm voice. "Some political pundits have dared say Father's madness has already begun to manifest in you. You leave Drakon for days, not one of your aides knows your schedule, you refuse to see even Ellie and me…"

"That's why you're all worried?" Andreas asked with a laugh. "That Theos gave me his madness in addition to everything else?"

Eleni spoke up. "Of course not. But we do think you've been acting strange. Andreas, the House of Tharius is waiting for your word to release news of your engagement. The coronation is in two months and you—"

His phone pinged and every nerve in him went on high alert. He knew even before he switched on his phone's screen what the news was going to be. His fingers shook when he swiped the screen.

Found the target. Sending location specs now.

His breath balled up in his chest, and he had to force himself to exhale.

Anticipation bubbled in his blood, coupled with savage satisfaction. "Let the House of Tharius know it's off."

The shock that spread through the huge room made the hairs on his neck rise. Nik and Eleni looked at him with such concern in their eyes that for the first time in months Andreas felt a little guilt. "I apologize for leaving you both in the lurch these past few months. I needed—"

"*Thee mou*, Andreas!" Nik burst out. "We don't care that for the first time in thirty-six years, you took a few months for yourself."

"Not the first time," he said automatically. "I took

a free year just when your health improved. Almost ten years ago."

Nikandros frowned. "When Theos tried to make me his leashed dog?"

"A few months before that happened, yes." When Andreas had, in a fit of madness, threatened Theo that he would walk out on Drakon if he didn't give him some time off.

"Andreas." Eleni reached him, her voice wavering. "You can't be crowned King without a wife. That's one of the oldest Drakonite laws. No member of the Crown Council will let you defy it. Are you…are you giving up the crown?"

Nikandros cursed so filthily that he had to laugh.

Andreas patted his sister's hand awkwardly. "I'm not doing any such thing, Eleni. I will be crowned as scheduled."

"You need a wife for that." Nik again. Only Gabriel stood silent, staring at him from those steel-grey eyes. Gabriel, his brother-in-law, who had figured out the truth.

"Whatever you're considering—" Eleni was close to tears now "—please tell us. Nik and I would never judge you for what—"

"I can't marry Maria Tharius because I already have a wife. For two years, I've been trying to locate her."

You are like me, Andreas, in every way. The same taste for power and control runs in your blood. Why do you think your little wife ran?

Those words had haunted him for two years now. But he didn't give a damn.

He would willingly be a monster if that meant she was back in his life.

"You're married? To whom? When? Why didn't you ever…" Eleni faintly shook with the force of her questions, until Gabriel put his hands on her shoulders and absorbed her petite form into his.

"She was Father's ward. I married her during that sabbatical year in a secret civil ceremony."

"Father had a ward?" Another curse from Nikandros, for he knew that meant another life his father would have played games with.

"Your pity is wasted on her, Nik," Andreas said stonily. "Turns out Father and she understood each other perfectly well."

"Ariana Sakis." Eleni pronounced the name that had become so much a part of his own makeup that Andreas couldn't remember a day before her life tangled with his. "She was shy of eighteen by a few months."

Utter shock was etched on their faces now.

He'd been twenty-six and he'd married a barely legal eighteen-year-old in a secret ceremony… He could have grown two horns and a tail and it would have been less shocking.

"Her parents…died in a car accident. There were rumors that they'd been arguing, that her mother had driven it into the tree on purpose," Eleni explained to Nik. "Her father…was a military general, a close friend of Father.

"There was a lot of talk about what an abusive husband he was and Father immediately severed the connection between the House of Drakos and him.

"Only a handful of people knew he had her custody and he sent her off to…no one knew where. I don't think she even set foot in the palace."

"To a fishing village off the coast," Andreas finished. "Having met Father a couple of times, she'd been more than willing to go."

"That's where you met her?" asked Nikandros.

Andreas nodded. "I… I demanded Father give me a year to do as I wanted, to research a book I wanted to write. He agreed, after a lot of ranting.

"Little did he know that I would end up at the same little village that summer."

Crisp mountain air, blue ponds surrounded by lush woods, a remote cabin, a single coffee shop…and a girl with copper-colored hair and a wide, impish smile.

Andreas swayed as the past reached into him with a clawed hand. Those months in that village with Ariana had been the most glorious of his life.

Too good to last, he realized now with a bitterness that choked him.

"If you married her, how come none of us met her? We didn't even know."

"Father and I decided to wait for a more opportune time to announce that I had wed. For the three months of our marriage, she stayed in an apartment ten miles from the palace."

"You've been looking for her…since Father's decline began." Eleni jerked her chin up. All the pieces were beginning to fall into place. "Where was she all these years, Andreas?"

"Father told me she died in a boating accident after I returned from that oil summit in the Middle East that year."

"Instead?" Nik asked the question, tension filling his shoulders.

"Instead, she took the ten million he offered, faked her death and disappeared under a new identity."

"That's…horrible." Eleni, always loyal to her brothers, had formed her opinion. "How could she make you think she was dead?"

Mia frowned. "You've found this woman now, haven't you?" Something almost like fear glittered in her tired gaze. "Andreas, what is it that you intend to do? Clearly, the woman has made her choice. All of Drakon's eyes will be on her."

It was an edict he'd heard since before he'd even hit puberty. All of the media's eyes would be on him and the woman he chose, Theos had whispered continuously.

She must bring either incomparable wealth—Gabriel's sister had met the first condition—or good breeding in her own blood—Maria Tharius had met both—or be a woman with powerful connections who would agree to become the perfectly ornamental Queen.

Ariana had been none of the above.

"You could divorce her." Gabriel spoke for the first time.

"Drakonite law mandates the couple wait for eighteen months after they file for divorce," Eleni supplied, frowning. "With the coronation in two months, he can't file for a divorce now."

Andreas smiled, uncaring what they all saw in his face. "Father, in his Machiavellian masterminding, assumed that her being officially dead was enough to terminate our marriage. But she's alive. So, even if I wanted, I could not marry Maria Tharius now.

"Ariana will be the next Queen of Drakon." The declaration fell from his mouth, resonated in the very air that filled the King's Palace.

He found he liked the sound of it. An additional bonus was that his father would be rolling in his grave.

Ariana stared at the white stone building of the small, beautiful church in downtown Fort Collins and shivered from head to toe. The frigid October wind that stole through her flimsy wedding dress had nothing to do with it.

The past would not leave her alone today. Didn't matter that it was over ten years since she had married Andreas Drakos, the Crown Prince of Drakon, in a little forgotten church in a backwater fishing village near the mountains.

Didn't matter that in a few hours she was to marry Magnus.

A vein of utter misery ran through her day and night.

She was Anna to her friends, to her colleagues at the legal aid agency where she worked, and to the little community she belonged to amidst the Rocky Mountains in Colorado.

Anna was not an impulsive, reckless woman that self-destructed in the name of love. Anna was not a woman who gave in to the dangerous passion for a man who didn't know how to love.

Instead Anna was supposed to be married this evening to a nice, understanding man. Her friends must be thinking she'd lost her mind. But she had needed to get away from the madness of it all. She'd barely eaten a morsel of food yesterday and nothing at the dinner their friends had arranged for her and Magnus.

Against every better instinct, she pulled her phone out of her coat jacket and compulsively opened a browser. The page was still open to the same article she'd been reading for the last month.

She perused it greedily, as if reading it for the hundredth time would somehow change the gist of it.

Crown Prince Andreas Drakos of Drakon was to announce his choice for his Queen, before his coronation as the King of Drakon, a tiny principality in the Mediterranean again making its mark in the financial world.

A woman who was regal and educated, a doyenne of charities, born to wealth and perfect bloodlines. A woman who would be soft and womanly, a perfect complement to his brooding, controlling masculinity.

She had known that Andreas would one day take another woman, a woman far more suitable than her, to be his wife, to be the Queen of Drakon. That he had waited this long at all, when she knew of his devotion to Drakon, was a shock in itself.

And yet, from the moment she'd seen the little article, her world had tilted on its axis.

Was Anna really any better than the impulsive hothead she had been then? Was there any other reason except that her heart had broken a little again when she'd seen news of Andreas's coronation and it had prompted her to accept Magnus's proposal?

Thee mou, was she willing to destroy Magnus's life, too?

Whatever sun had been shining this morning had receded under dark clouds, the weather resonating her own dark thoughts. She had to break it off. Before she hurt Magnus, before...

The smooth swish of a finely tuned engine broke her focus.

She looked up and froze, wishing with every cell inside of her that she could truly freeze, become invisible, blend into the gray, leaf-bare trees around her. Could become one of the statues that littered the lovely town.

The pounding of her heart in her ears said she was far too alive.

For she recognized the little black-and-gold flag fluttering in the harsh wind on the hood of the European luxury car idling not two steps away. She knew the symbol of the golden dragon with fires spewing out of its wide jaws. She knew the man inside and his body and he knew hers, better than she did her own.

Legs quaking under her, she stumbled away from the curving stone wall that led to the steps of the church. Wrapped her arm around a tall tree for support.

Every primal instinct she possessed screamed at her to run, to flee. And yet not a single cell obeyed. Not a single muscle moved even as she heard the click of the car door, even as she saw polished black shoes step out of the car, even as the tall angular form straightened.

He'd found her.

Dear God, after ten years, he'd caught up to her. Just as she had always known he would, in the deep dark of the night when she couldn't hold the memories at bay.

Crown Prince Andreas Drakos, soon to be King of Drakon, was here.

A long black coat fluttered around his ankles, wavy hair the color of a raven's wing carelessly combed away from a high forehead. Power stamped across those high cheekbones, the patrician nose, the thin-lipped mouth. Arrogant entitlement and self-confidence dripped from him with every movement of his body.

Jet-black eyes, hard and flinty like glittering opals, eyes that reflected nothing back, eyes that had sometimes felt as if there was nothing behind them, swept over her shivering body and came to rest on her face. "*Kalimera*, Ariana."

Their eyes collided and held, sending a tsunami of emotions racing through her body. God, those eyes...she had drowned in them once. She had reveled in making them glow with humor, in making them darken in passion, in trying to break through that opaque shield.

She pressed her bare hands against the rough bark of the tree, hoping to jerk some kind of self-preservation instinct into life, for some kind of rationality to master the sheer emotional assault she was under.

Hands tucked into the pockets of his trousers, clad in all black, he looked like a dark angel come to serve swift justice. "It does not seem like a good day to be getting married. Does it, *pethi mou*?"

So he knew.

Ariana licked her dry lips, swallowing away the knowledge that she'd been about to call it off. Her gut instinct had been right. "What...what are you doing here?"

"Here on this side of the pond, in Colorado, in this little wonderful town that you've been hiding in?" He didn't move, nor did a muscle flicker in his face. In that deep, gravelly voice of his, he could have been inquiring after the bitter weather.

They could have been a couple of friends discussing

trivialities. No anger or emotion fractured his cool expression. Only a faint thread of sarcasm bled through.

"Or here in front of this beautiful little church on this bleary afternoon where you're waiting for the man you're supposed to marry in a few hours? Should I answer the general or the specific?"

Ariana closed her eyes. Didn't help one bit. His presence was a hum of power in the air, making something in her vibrate in tune. Dragging cold air deep into her lungs, she flicked her eyes open. Feeling was beginning to come back into her muscles. And along with it memories and an unholy amount of panic.

How had she forgotten that the smoother Andreas's voice got, the hotter his rage? The deeper the fracture in his self-control, the colder and calmer his actions? It was his shut-down mode, where neither reason nor begging would filter through. Fresh wind made her eyes water. It had to be the wind. "I don't have your magic with words, Andreas."

He inclined his head in a regal nod. "I am to be King soon. I thought now would be a wise time to take care of the little business between us. After all, you ran out on me without a word, and who knows when you will decide you want to come back to me?"

Shivers raced down her spine. "Go back to your precious Drakon." She couldn't help the bitterness in her voice, even as she cautioned herself against it. "You have nothing to worry about with me. You and I—" her voice caught, and still, nothing changed in his expression "—were an episode from a different life. The media will never catch hold of our little story, neither will I claim even an acquaintance.

"Ariana Sakis, for all intents and purposes, is dead."

She glanced up and her breath seized in her lungs.

Suddenly, he was there in front of her, blocking everything else from her vision. Blocking the entire world from her. Sandalwood, flared by his body's heat, taunted her nostrils. Filled her with sensations and memories. Such an interestingly warm scent for a man whose blood was decidedly cold. But then his passion had been just as contrasting to the ruthless lack of his heart.

"Ariana Drakos," he corrected with the faintest trace of warning. "Do not forget you belong to me."

Nothing so tacky as a raised voice or a teetering temper from the House of Drakos.

"You might be King of your bloody palace, Andreas—" panic rushed reckless words to her mouth "—but not of me. Magnus will be here any minute and I won't—"

"Your fiancé has been made aware of the situation and is not coming."

So polite even as he stood there, playing havoc with her life. So infuriatingly calm. Her hands itched to muss up that perfectly placid expression of his. The devil in her burned to unsettle him as he did her. That urge was dangerous. Just being near Andreas was like throwing herself off a cliff—exhilarating and terrifying. And she had stopped doing that to herself a long time ago.

"What the hell did you tell Magnus?"

"That he should call it quits while his life is still under his control."

"Is this what you have sunk to? Chasing away the man in my life? Have you become as low and manipulative as your father then, Andreas?"

His jaw tightened. "I didn't have to chase him, Ariana. Like any sensible man, Magnus seemed uninclined toward being the other party in bigamy. In fact, he sounded angry at your deception."

"Bigamy?" She covered the distance between them without caring. Her heart seemed to slow down in her chest, a dreadful cold filling her. "What do you mean, bigamy?"

His mouth relaxed, he stood waiting against the same tree as if he had all the time in the world. As if there was nothing that would give him more pleasure than to watch the ground being pulled away from under her. As if he'd planned and lived this moment a thousand times and he couldn't let his enjoyment end.

She shook her grip on his coat but he didn't budge. "What do you mean?"

A smile curved his mouth. Rendering him starkly beautiful. "My father and you missed one small detail in your plan. If I had never discovered you were alive, it wouldn't have mattered so much.

"But I did."

"What detail?" she was shouting now, her voice lost in the gray bleakness around her. Everything about those few days was still jumbled in her head. She'd been acting on pure animal instincts—fear the overriding one—and listening to King Theos had been the worst kind of mistake.

All she'd wanted was to escape Drakon before Andreas came back from his summit. Before she was caught in the web of her own love for him.

She'd been so naive that she had played right into Theos's manipulative hands. But Andreas wouldn't believe her now.

Her leaving him had been a betrayal to a man who didn't break rules for anyone, an unforgivable mistake to a man whose word meant everything to him.

She clasped his jaw, forcing him to look at her. "What detail, Andreas?"

He still didn't hold her. Didn't touch her in any way. Those eyes trapped her again, until even breathing was a chore. Those eyes betrayed all his emotions—fury, shock and the cold enjoyment of her fate now. "The papers you signed for Theos, dissolving our marriage, he never presented them to me.

"Your supposed death bought him time and then... I don't know what he and you planned. I never saw those papers until a few months ago. The motion didn't even get filed in court.

"You are still my wife."

CHAPTER TWO

SHEER TERROR FILLED her eyes as she stared at him. "Your wife?" she repeated, as if she couldn't think past those two words.

Andreas studied her greedily, his skin prickling with that sensation only Ariana could arouse.

Her lips were dry, trembling. Her copper gold hair, her crowning glory, was tied into that messy knot she'd always put it in, complaining that it was too much. Her cheekbones were sharp and high, forever giving her that malnourished look. Her skin was still that golden shade though it looked alarmingly pale just then.

"You and I are still married, Ariana. Ten years and going strong. Except for the little problem of you wanting to marry another man."

Her fingers became lax around his coat, her body trembling with tension. "Ariana is dead," she kept repeating through pale lips.

Words that had haunted him for eight years.

He had imagined her death a hundred different ways, a million different times. He had hated himself for leaving her with his father. He had been through hell and back because he thought he hadn't protected her.

He fisted his hands by his sides, fighting the urge to

wrap his hands around her. Fighting the overwhelming impulse to push her against the tree and crush her mouth with his.

Because to see Ariana was to want Ariana. He didn't remember a time he hadn't wanted to possess her with that raw longing.

And yet lust was only a pale shadow behind the need to ensure that she was alive and not a figment of his imagination, a flimsy shadow from his feverish nightmares.

Outwardly, she hadn't changed at all.

Thin, angular body built with lean muscle. Wide, brown-ringed eyes too big for her gamine face. Sharp, bladelike nose followed by a mouth so lushly pillowy, so poutingly full, that no man could see it and not think dirty, lustful thoughts.

It was as if all the austerity that had been executed in her face had to be made up for in that mouth.

She looked just as common and nondescript as Theos had called her back then.

Only her eyes had changed.

That twinkle that had made them glow, as if she held the glorious flicker of life itself inside her, it was gone. Wariness filled them now. He wanted to shove her away from him, stop her from touching him like she used to do.

But the damage to his system was already done.

His body roared to life at the soft imprint she left with hers. Long, toned legs tangled with his, her body trembling faintly against his. The scent of her—just her skin and the lavender soap she apparently still used—invaded his bloodstream. Like Pavlov's dog, every cell inside him stood to attention. Memories and sensations of pleasure and something else, a sense of being utterly alive, poured into his skin, making him heated.

"This is your petty revenge on me," she finally whispered, her mouth only inches apart from his. A loud thrum began under his skin. "Your way of playing with my life while you announce your own marriage to the world. You will let me dangle at your fingertips, holding this ridiculous threat over my head.

"Because I had the temerity to walk away from the controlling, arrogant, ruthless man you are, Andreas."

He scowled. "You think it was my pride that was dented by your betrayal, by your lies?"

"Yes," she said defiantly. "For you're not capable of feeling anything else."

Andreas flinched, her words landing like barbed fists on his flesh. *Thee mou*, it seemed even now, when she was utterly in the wrong, she dared to challenge him, dared to call him out for her mistakes.

"You could have done this through your lawyers. You could have sent me the divorce papers through one of your lackeys. But no…you had to do it personally because you couldn't forego the pleasure of ruining my life before you go back to rule your bloody kingdom."

"You're mistaken again, Ariana. I did not come simply to ruin your engagement."

"Then why are you here?"

"For two years, since Father let it slip that you were alive, I've been waiting for this moment.

"I will be crowned King of Drakon soon and I need my wife by my side. I have come to take you home to Drakon."

Her gaze searched his, desperate. What little fight

had been there seemed to deflate out of her. As if she was shrinking right in front of his eyes. "You've got to be kidding me."

He touched her then, tracing the delicate line of her jaw with the tip of his forefinger. Her skin was silky smooth to his touch, a faint tremor running through it. "But you already know I have no sense of humor."

"You…can't…" her breath came in little gasps "…do…this."

Her thin body going slack against him, his wife did what she'd always forced him to do. She fainted and forced him to catch her. Forced him to hold her fragile body in his, before he was ready for any such contact. Feeling fear, and panic and a hundred other emotions that he'd never had encountered otherwise.

Her gown's bodice was so tight that Andreas drew his pocket knife out of his coat and cut the front off. The blue tinge around her mouth began to recede, his own panic fading with it.

He easily lifted her slender form and made his way to the waiting car, icy anger thawing and giving way to shock.

She might not have changed outwardly but there was something different about her. Something fragile and fractured. Almost as if there was a piece missing.

He'd expected a radiant, carefree bride, ready to ride into another adventure with another man she'd sucked in with her effervescent personality, with her vivacity and wit. He'd expected her to be living it up in some party town with the money she'd taken from his father.

He hadn't expected this…this *waif*, with bruises under her eyes, working away all hours at a nonprofit legal agency. She made barely any money. She shared a one-bedroom apartment, the size of his closet, with another woman. He'd have never believed that silly, rebellious girl would have the interest to study law much less the grit to get a degree and practice.

Barely out of breath, he slowly lowered her into the seat and slid into place next to her.

Every savage promise he'd made himself that he'd make her suffer crumbled as he gathered her body into his.

Once again, all his plans turned to dust by the infuriating woman.

Just as she had been able to make him laugh, make him long for something he had never known back then. Make him lose his mind in the desperate need to possess her.

All through that summer, Ariana had wielded some kind of magic over him.

That laughing, reckless girl had shattered through to his core, given him a taste of an unparalleled joy he'd never known.

And so he'd done the unthinkable and married her when it had been time to leave. Possessing Ariana had equaled holding that joy in the palm of his hand. It had meant being something more than the Crown Prince, something he hadn't even realized he'd needed to be until then.

He had forgotten who and what he was, he had clung desperately to that feeling, had thought it enough to have her in his life.

Except it hadn't been enough for her.

With that same recklessness that had lured him to

her, she had destroyed their lives. It was that same girl he had expected to find today.

But she was right.

This was not the Ariana he had met that summer, the Ariana he had married.

And yet, letting her go was not an option.

Ariana came awake slowly, her throat parched, her mind blank. Air filled her in quick, choppy bursts.

"Drink this."

Ignoring the questions buzzing through her head, she took the bottle and drank the water. It was cold and crisp, what she desperately needed.

"Iedas Mountain Springs," the label on the water bottle said, with a small sketch of the majestic mountain range in Drakon... *Drakon!*

She jerked upright. Cream leather walls greeted her, understated luxury permeating the ambience. Soft lights from the ceiling cast a golden glow around the cabin.

Cabin... She was in the rear cabin of a private jet—a jet that belonged to the blasted House of Drakos.

The events of the afternoon came back in a fast reel.

Andreas had said they were still married.

Andreas had said he was going to take her back to Drakon.

Andreas had caught her when she'd fainted.

The panic felt like ants crawling all over her skin. She pushed her legs out and stood up. The cabin tilted but she had to get out of here.

The slither of her dress, her wedding dress, alerted her. She looked down, found the corset cut neatly down in the middle. The beaded bodice hung open through the center, gaping open to reveal her slip and the shadow of her breasts.

Ariana held it up with both hands and forced her Jell-O legs to move.

Before she took another step, he was before her.

A man as hard as the rock on which his palace sat. Yet, as she looked at him now, there were white lines around his mouth, and he was not so solid.

"Why am I here? What is that sound?"

"They're readying for takeoff."

"No!"

"Sit down, Ariana."

"Get out of my way."

"You're in no shape to go anywhere."

"I swear, Andreas, if you don't move out of my way—"

His fingers gripped her arms, exerting pressure backward. "Calm down before you faint again!"

"How dare you? You bastard!" Ariana let her hand fly.

The crack of her palm against his cheek was like a pop of thunder, leaving an utter silence behind. She clutched her wrist with her left hand, shock jarring it. Breathing hard, she looked up.

He hadn't even touched his jaw. Except for the tight clench of it, the little jerk of his head, he showed no reaction to what she'd done. He still supported her.

"Does that conclude this episode to your satisfaction, Ari?"

Her shortened name made her breath catch. "I will not apologize."

He shrugged.

That casual gesture was like fuel to her rage.

"You're kidnapping me. Really?" She fisted her hands and went at him, lost to all reason. "After all the propriety and decorum and a hundred other rules you demand of everyone, you're actually kidnapping me?"

Of course it was exactly what he had planned. And Ariana had so nicely played into his hands, by literally fainting at his feet.

Damn it, Ari.

"You will not like it if I subdue you on the bed, Ari. Or maybe you will, since we both know what will happen the moment I lie on top of you." The cold matter-of-factness of his threat made everything still in her.

Ariana turned and met his inscrutable gaze, wrapping her mind around this.

"Should we put my theory to the test or shall you calm down?"

"Let me go."

He did instantly. With an urgency that made her flush.

Her legs simply gave out and Ariana slid into a graceless heap on the bed.

This had been coming, Ari, a nauseating voice whispered. *You just buried your head in the sand. You knew he was going to catch up with you one day.*

She didn't know how long they sat like that. She on the bed, trying to catch her breath, trying to quell the panic, and he sitting in the one armchair in the corner, watching her.

A lion crouching in silence, waiting for his prey to show weakness.

The long coat and jacket were gone. Replaced by a white designer dress shirt with a white undershirt— nothing so scandalous as going without one for the uptight Crown Prince of Drakon—and black custom-made trousers for his six-four height. Dark olive skin at his throat beckoned to her. She followed the trail of the chain around his neck with her eyes.

His dog tags from his time in the Drakonite Army, where he'd trained from fifteen to eighteen, would be under that undershirt. Platinum cufflinks. A platinum-plated watch glinted on his left wrist. Black Italian handmade shoes gleamed where he'd folded one foot on top of his thigh.

The soft lightning of the cabin wreathed his face in shadows, showing the sharp planes and hollows of his face to perfection.

He was leaner than she remembered and it made him look even more distant and withdrawn. There were lines on his face now, especially around that thinly sculpted mouth. At twenty-six he'd been gorgeous in an uptight, starchy kind of way.

Ten years later now, he seemed even more comfortable in his skin. Even more arrogant and ruthless about his place in the world.

Every small thing she noticed brought back a memory thudding into her conscious, as physical as a blow to her solar plexus. Her throat dried promptly again, her heart forever in that lurching rhythm when he was near.

Slowly the impact of this, *of him*, hit her in its completion. She wasn't running away from this, not yet at least.

No, there was no running away at all from this, she corrected herself. Not unless she wanted him to give her chase for the rest of their lives.

Realizing she'd been gaping at him, she pulled her

gaze up. Chin propped against his fist, he raised a brow. He didn't tease her for gawking at him like a teenager.

He didn't need the validation to his masculinity, to his ego.

Power was second skin to him, women flocked to him like buzzing bees. Actresses and models, CEOs and princesses, women had been falling at his feet since puberty. If he'd been merely one more vacant, lazy royal out to have a good time, maybe he wouldn't have so much pull.

But no, Andreas Drakos was smart as a whip. A historian, an army veteran, a weaver of words. *Christos*, there wasn't anything he didn't excel at.

And yet he'd chosen her.

She frowned, the question had tormented her for years, struggled into a comfortable position and took stock of her body. A leaf fluttering in a harsh gale would have more strength than her at the moment.

Of all the stupid, moronic things to do in front of this man… She pressed a hand to her temple.

She felt the heat of his body instantly in the air around the bed. Whatever reprieve she'd gotten was over.

In silent scrutiny, he fluffed the pillows and propped them against the wall, and then pulled her into a sitting position. With economic movements, his fingers barely touching her, he arranged the duvet around her. Gave her another bottle of water that she emptied within seconds.

Hysteria began to bubble up through her throat and she laughed. Water spurted out of her nose and mouth inelegantly, and he promptly wiped her nose and mouth with a napkin. On and on went her near manic laughter until tears streamed out from her eyes. Until the ball of tension that had lodged in her chest since she'd seen him standing in front of the church slowly deflated.

He raised a brow again.

"How many women can claim Crown Prince Andreas Drakos waited on them like a lowly member of staff?" she quipped, perfectly understanding his question.

A sudden tightness gripped her chest. Wordless communication had been so their thing.

"So you still possess that ridiculous sense of humor."

She tensed as he sat down at the edge of the bed. Not near enough to touch, yet tantalizingly close. Her body couldn't take this much heightened awareness after what had been a drought of ten years. Not for long, not without combusting with need.

"What the hell was that?"

"Be glad I didn't scratch that perfect face. Or maybe I should have. A little imperfection would have at least made you look human."

A jagged sigh. An echo of all the times Ari had pushed his buttons. "I speak of your fainting."

"You showed up after ten years and I fainted." She sighed. *Regression much, Ari?*

"Continue like that and it will only confirm my belief that you're still that reckless, juvenile, rebellious brat I knew back then."

"What can I say? You bring out the worst in me, Your Highness."

Their eyes sought each other instantly.

Are you my watchdog, Your Highness?

Crack a smile, Your Highness.

It's called a vodka shot, Your Highness.

Had she been that naive, that foolish to have teased this man like that? Had he actually let her?

"Ariana, focus." It wasn't even a warning. Just a smidgen of his impatience leaking. "If I hadn't been there, you would have been on the grass, in the cold, for God knows how long. Is this your new thing now, fainting?"

"New thing?"

"Yes. Pot brownies, vodka shots, fasting for days to lose weight… *Christos*, do I need to go on? You were always ridiculously reckless about your well-being."

Ari massaged her temples with her fingers. He was right.

She had thrown herself into her sudden, boundless freedom, as naively as jumping off a cliff. Guilt over her parents' deaths had stolen reason from her. The need to experience life to the fullest after seventeen years of being trapped in a golden cage…it had consumed her.

He'd thought her ditzy, willful, reckless and any number of even less complimentary things. She had been all those and more. But not in the past ten years, not anymore.

Her hands settled on her belly, corrosive grief scratching her throat.

The freedom she'd finally got, the need to make something of her life, it had come at such a high price. But it had helped her find herself, helped her achieve control over those impulses that would destroy her.

Until this past month when his impending announcement had undone her again. And that made fear whisper through her bones. It was the same circle of self-abuse her mother had been stuck in with her father.

"Ariana?"

"I…had a salad for lunch yesterday and nothing since then. It has been a stressful week—the caseload at the firm is crazy right now and then a doubly stressful morning. I've never fainted before." Except that one time after she had left Drakon and him behind. Because in her recklessness, the same that he accused her of right now, it had taken a fainting spell to realize she'd been three months pregnant.

His instant control of the situation, his interrogation of her as if she were a child, grated like nothing else. But to be fair, that's what she had been then. "Because of the elevation above sea level of this town, I sometimes find it hard to breathe."

"Mountain air makes your asthma worse. I checked your little purse and you didn't have your inhaler on you."

She looked up then and swallowed. She'd thought he would delete anything related to their time together from his life, from his mind. At least after learning of the biggest lie she'd ever told.

Apparently, like her, Andreas had forgotten nothing of their time together. Of their short-lived marriage. Of how they made each other burn up in flames when they touched, and ruined each other when they didn't.

"It does flare it up from time to time. But it makes up with everything else."

A little frown appeared between his brows. "Makes up?"

"The fact that it flares my asthma is a little inconvenience to what I have found here. I…found a community here, Andreas. My life has meaning here. There are women who count on me." She held his gaze, air ballooning up in her chest, smothering her lungs. Time to face the facts. "You can't really mean what you said earlier."

"Have you ever known me to say anything I didn't mean?"

No. He'd never once said that he loved her, even in the throes of passion, even when he'd let his control slip. And it was something to watch the iron-control-clad, emotionless, uptight Crown Prince lose it in the sheets.

She swung her legs out of the bed and stood up slowly. When he neared her to offer assistance with clear reluctance—because of course every touch and look had to be calculated in that steel trap that was his mind—she held him off with her hand.

The cut corset of her wedding dress hung limply around her waist but Ariana didn't care. She didn't care one bit what her sheer slip showed.

She didn't care that his gaze traveled all over her, noted her defiant pose, and yet didn't betray anything.

He had unraveled her life all over again and she was not going to hide and feel shame about it. She had to face Andreas and whatever came now, if she ever wanted to move forward in her life.

"Think about what you're proposing, Andreas. Your father was right in one thing—I hardly possess the bloodlines. I was never brought up to be the next Queen of Drakon.

"You…completely agreed with him." It took no

small amount of effort to put this forward rationally. "You… The moment we left the village…"

"What about it, Ariana?"

He had regretted what he'd done, she knew. But the past was done, useless. "Do you think I would be any more malleable this time around?" She lifted her chin. "The last ten years have only made me realize how right I was. We would have destroyed each other if I'd stayed."

He reached her then. Breath serrated her throat as he lifted his hand and softly clasped her jaw. For one sheer, indefinable moment, a wealth of emotion danced in his jet-black gaze. Pure rage and something else. A bleakness?

"Silly Ari. Do you think I give a damn about what you want or need right now?

"Your death tormented me for eight years.

"The little slip from Theos's mouth that you were not only alive, but that you took money from him to disappear—" tight lines emerged around his mouth, a small fracture in his control "—that news has tortured me for the last two years."

Ariana stared, stunned. A dent to his ego, she'd expected. But for Andreas to admit that losing her had tormented him…it was akin to the sun revolving around the earth. The pithy declaration raged through her, kindling feelings she couldn't handle.

Had he truly felt something for her then?

"This is exactly what your father wanted you to become."

"Theos is dead, *agapita*," he said softly, a wicked gleam in his eyes. "It has been years since his will, his word, has had the power to move me. The power to persuade me. The power to control me.

"I have become my own man, Ari. Isn't that what you wanted long ago?"

She'd have given anything to hear that ten years ago. But not anymore. "The moment we land in Drakon, I'll yell what you've done through the rooftops. Your image can't survive a scandal."

He bared his teeth in a feral smile. "So you have kept tabs on me."

The sound that fell from her mouth was half growl, half screech. "I know my place even in the illustrious world that you're the unrivaled lord of. One word from me will plunge the House of Drakos into a horrible scandal."

"Do you really want to threaten me?"

Panic bloomed, making her voice rise. "My entire life is here. Even more importantly, my clients are here."

"Your fiancé fell over himself in his haste to accept my conditions. He gets to keep the legal agency running and keeps quiet about your secret identity for the rest of his life."

"I built that agency with my blood and tears." The one good thing that had come out of the loss she'd suffered.

"You built it with the dirty payoff you took from my father. Even your education was paid for by the House of Drakos. And since we're still married—"

"Half of everything I own is yours," she finished. Her mind whirled. "And you need Magnus to keep quiet about where I've been and what I've been doing."

His jaw clenched and Ariana exhaled roughly. Finally, there was one point she could negotiate with. But he didn't give her even that chance.

"Your clients, what do you think will happen if the media gets hold of who you truly are? That you've been living a lie for ten years."

"It's not a lie. I busted my ass to earn my law degree. I opened that nonprofit legal aid agency because I wanted to help those women."

"And when the world finds out that you're not Anna Harris but Ariana Drakos, wife of the King of Drakon—"

"My clients will be dragged into the limelight along with me." She exhaled roughly. "Those are women who have already been abused by men they trusted. Which will keep me quiet. Am I getting close, Andreas?"

He smiled then—a jagged mockery that made her chest ache. "You know what I find truly hard to believe in this new, peachy life you've made for yourself?"

"What?" She snarled the question at him.

"Am I to believe that you have found your true, deep purpose in your scattered life finally? That you truly devote yourself tirelessly to those women and their plight?"

If there was a moment that Ariana truly wanted to sink her nails into that perfect, arrogant, condescending face and scratch it, it was then. Ten years of striving to make something of herself, to give meaning to what she'd lost, to make a meaningful path for herself, and his careless disdain crushed it all.

And he knew it. He was all but challenging her to launch herself at him again, to go back to that lowest denominator of herself she'd once thrived on.

She would attack him and he would subdue her... and it would lead to only one conclusion. The knowledge suffused the very air around them with a dense heat.

Every time they had fought in those horrible three months of their marriage, they'd ended up in bed. Or against the wall. Or on the chaise longue with the Crown Prince on his knees, with his arrogant head between her thighs.

The memory shimmered like a bright glitter in his coal-black eyes.

With the sheer will that had helped her survive through the darkest night of her life, Ari looked away. Air rushed into her lungs, clearing the haze.

Her biggest defense against Andreas was to show leaving him hadn't been a whim. That she wasn't a car crash in the making anymore. That she had come into her own strength these last ten years. That she'd proactively made something of her life.

"I care about my clients, about their privacy, about not turning everything Magnus and I worked for into a lie. So, yes, you win my silence. But nothing else."

"How refreshing that you're capable of loyalty, even if it's toward another man, *pethi mou*. I told him, soon enough you'd have found a reason to run out on him. That your precious freedom would have come calling.

"Is it not your pattern?"

Ariana flinched, the softly delivered statement even more painful for she'd been about to do exactly the same thing to Magnus. Not for some kind of femme fatale reason but because she'd realized Magnus deserved much better than her.

"I didn't think you of all people would be crass

enough to typecast me as some kind of vacant-headed, freewheeling slut. If for no other reason than that it would taint your own pristine image, your own association with me."

"What does that mean?"

"I was eighteen, Andreas. I… I was bowled over by you. I threw myself at you. I was…messed up after my parents' deaths, and you were a high unlike anything I'd ever known.

"You were—you *are* unlike any other man I've ever known.

"Jesus, did you know what your attention, your reluctant interest, meant to me? You…who didn't show interest in princesses, and models and CEOs.

"You looked at me. *Me*—messed-up, frightened, guilty Ariana.

"You married me knowing who and what I was. So, if we have to call out someone for the…*twisted* mess that was our marriage, it's you."

"Was that the justification when you let me think you had died in a horrible drowning accident," he bit out and she flinched. "Maybe I will let you go, Ariana. Maybe one of these days I will find that little bit of decency within myself again. Maybe you can go back to being Anna Harris and the savior of those women in your little town again."

And in those statements of his, Ariana saw his shredded control for what it was. Saw his loathing that she was still an obsession with him. He despised himself, and her, because he couldn't give her up.

Any hopes she had of convincing him perished in that moment. After all, she did know him better than anyone.

"So this is about revenge?"

"Call it whatever the hell you want to." His gaze tracked her face and her torn clothes. He fisted his hand so tight by his side that the knuckles were white.

For the first time that day, Ariana realized how tremendous his self-control was.

"You need food and rest. Do not force me to manhandle you into that, too. We both know whether it will be pleasure or punishment."

Ariana fell onto the bed with a soft thud, the recrimination in his eyes burning through her like acid. Her skin still prickling, for the first time since she'd known him, she was grateful for his iron-clad self-control.

Because, even after all these years, she had none when it came to resisting the Crown Prince of Drakon.

CHAPTER THREE

"MRS. DRAKOS? YOUR HIGHNESS?"

For the second time in a few hours, Ariana jerked upright so suddenly that her neck gave a painful twinge. She looked at the stewardess patiently waiting for her to wake up.

So the cat was out of the bag.

Instead of the panic she braced herself for, all she felt was a…quiet resignation. Not the give-up-and-become-his-wife kind. But the guilty-as-hell kind.

Whatever he had done to her, however much she had despised him at the end of their marriage, it was clear that she had miscalculated the effect of her supposed death on Andreas. On hearing of his swift engagement to a real estate mogul's sister, her own guilt had been alleviated.

She didn't belong in the Crown Prince's world and that he'd replaced her so fast had been proof enough.

Of course, that miscalculation had been aided by his father.

If Andreas had grieved her loss, who knew how Theos had twisted that to his advantage?

King Theos, she had realized within a week of meeting her guardian as her father-in-law, had possessed an unhealthy hold on his heir. He'd seen her as nothing but a weakness to eliminate from his son's life.

What had been painful was from the moment he had presented her to King Theos, even Andreas had begun to see her as that—a weakness to be hidden away.

The stewardess's eyes traveled over Ari's hair, which could rival the Amazon forest for its wildness right now, to the torn dress she had fallen asleep in.

Ari cringed. She stood up from the bed, and pushed the dress off her shoulders and hips.

Ill-concealed curiosity scampered across the woman's face. "I will take care of the dress, Your Highness. Have it mended. I'm sure you'd want to—"

"No, that's not necessary," Ari replied, pulling the slip off her shoulders. Her strapless bra stuck to the underside of her breasts uncomfortably, thanks to her habit of smothering herself under the covers. She stepped out of the slip seconds before the woman took it, almost dislodging Ari off her feet.

"Have it burned," a soft voice commanded from the entrance.

The need to cover herself was instinctive, self-preservation at its primal. Shaking, Ariana covered her midriff with her arms.

The stewardess had that look again, switching between her and Andreas, as if she could figure out the secret as to how this average-looking, falling-apart-at-the-seams waif had snared the most powerful, gorgeous man in Drakon.

It was a question the whole world was going to ask this time, not just King Theos, if Andreas had his way.

His gaze dipped past Ari's face this time—as if he'd

given himself permission to look, to linger—moved to the pulse beating wildly at her neck, betraying the sudden tension that suffused her every cell, to the curves of her breasts rising and falling. A languorous ache settled low in her belly, her nipples hard against the flimsy bra.

"Checking up on me already?" Fear of how just one look from him turned her on destroyed the need for discretion in front of a member of the staff. "There's no way to escape, unless you're willing to provide me with a parachute. You can see me plummet to death, at least."

He closed his eyes, his chest barely lifted and fell with his exhale, and then leveled that black gaze at her again. Military precision to every single breath. "I came in to see if you were awake. Petra needs your prescription for your inhaler. I will not have you fainting everywhere."

"Petra?"

"Yes, my secretary." He looked down at his phone, frowned, typed a message and looked up again.

Tall, blonde, with a voluptuous body, armed with a master's from a renowned university in Drakon, and hailing from a highly connected Drakonite family. Andreas's oldest friend and shadow. Theos's spy. If Ariana could give a form to all her self-doubts and insecurities back then, it would be Petra Cozakis. "I know Petra runs your life. And for the last time, it was the stress of the last week and that dress that did it today.

"Do not treat me as if I am still an imbecile, Andreas."

He raised a brow. Confirmation enough that that

was exactly how she was acting. "Petra is on this flight. Let her know if you need anything."

"No," she said loudly.

His gaze pinned her. "Precisely what are you saying no to?"

"If you're dragging me to the King's Palace, it will be different this time. I will not be hidden away like some stain on the great House of Drakos. I will not let your uptight, snobbish staff run circles around me. I will not communicate through your minions, will not let you pawn me off on them as if I was a thing to be managed." Maybe what Andreas needed was a dose of reality. For his staff and his family and the world to realize who he had chosen and how unsuitable she was.

Lines formed between his brows. "Leave us," he said to the stewardess without moving his gaze from Ariana.

The woman froze in the process of folding the damned dress. She thought Ariana and Andreas had gotten married in that dress, Ariana realized.

"Burn. That. Dress," he repeated. The stewardess nodded and scurried out.

Arms still around her waist, Ariana turned, grabbed the duvet and pulled it around her like a shroud. However she tried, the choice was to either cover her chest or her midriff.

She covered her midriff. Her bra was enough for her meager breasts. It wasn't like he hadn't seen the little she had to offer before.

The small scar she bore above her pubic bone might not be visible in the soft light, but she couldn't take the chance. Closing her eyes, she willed the grief down. The situation with Andreas was explosive enough without adding her discovery *after* she had left him that she'd been pregnant.

That she had lost her precious little baby boy was an unbearable, ever-present weight on her soul. For Andreas, it would only mean more betrayal. Worse, the loss of a *potential heir*, a figurehead to represent the House of Drakos's future.

Ariana couldn't bear to hear his dismissal of that tiny life. The guilt of it, the grief of it was all her own.

At least, it served as a reminder that she couldn't chance a pregnancy again.

Because there was no point in denying that she was going to end up in his bed. The attraction between them, it seemed, had survived despite everything.

She took a Post-it note and pen from the small bedstead and scribbled the name and number of her GP. Shards of glass seemed to be stuck in her throat when she turned. "I also need the prescription for my birth control pills filled."

The memory of their last fight, the bitterest and dirtiest of them all, sculpted sharp grooves in his already gaunt cheeks. His hesitation was like handing her a live grenade. Bulky duvet and all, she reached him, her heart threatening to rip out of her chest. "Have something to say, Andreas?"

As if pulled from the past, he slowly looked down at her. "No. Even I'm not cruel enough to bring a child into this. At least not anymore."

"Does that mean you intend to let me go at some point?"

This time, his answer was more thoughtful than driven by fury. "No."

"But isn't my only duty as your wife to produce as

many healthy heirs as soon as humanly possible? My purpose, to be your broodmare?"

Deep grooves etched on the sides of his mouth as he responded without inflection. "Nikandros's twins will be heirs."

"Of course," she said, swallowing away the ache. She had no idea why she was pushing him like this. Only that she wanted to hurt him as she was hurting. "How does the timeline look then? Do I have enough time to find a new GP in Drakon and get my pills without Petra and the entire palace knowing my business?"

His chin tilted down. "What?"

"The sex, Andreas? You and me and the humiliating sex that we're going to have, you have a timeline for that, right?

"Sex is your weapon in this revenge scheme, *ne*? The thing I could never refuse you, the thing that you threatened to hold against—" Her voice broke, and he...his features paled. "So, yeah, if your schedule allows me to wait, then you don't have to ask your secretary to fill your wife's birth control prescription."

When she'd have turned away from him, he gripped her arms so tightly that Ari knew she'd have bruises tomorrow. But the pain was worth the satisfaction that she had finally, finally ruffled him. "Humiliating sex? Punishment sex?" He turned her until she was facing him, her duvet forgotten, her stomach tying itself in knots. "Have you convinced yourself that with my power and prestige, I somehow forced you?

"Have you conveniently twisted the truth in that too, *agapita*? That you gave your innocence unwillingly?"

Laughter fell from her mouth, serrated and strange.

"No, it was never that, whatever it was." Her nose rubbed against his biceps, her mouth curving into a smile against the fabric of his shirt. Faint tension emanated from him, making Ari throw caution to the wind. "Even in this we disagree, *ne*, Andreas?"

He looked at her as though he was afraid she was going mad. She was a little afraid of that herself. "How?"

"To this day, I'm convinced that I seduced you and you're convinced that you seduced me. Even in this, we have a power struggle."

He didn't outright laugh. The rigid, sculpted curve of his thin lips didn't even move. But his grip on her arms eased. Something softened in his black eyes. A flash of that dry humor she had seen back then. Only she.

He lifted a finger and touched the tip of her nose. Her breath suspended in her throat, for Ari had a feeling he had been about to touch her mouth and changed his mind at the last second.

He'd been tempted. And it filled her with a heady power she didn't want.

"It was not so much a power struggle as it was you defying me. Defying everything I stood for—Drakon, the Palace, the House of Drakos, my father and me." His tone became far off, as if he too was reliving those first heady months when they had met.

Memories permeated the very air around them.

The first day he'd arrived at the café, he'd introduced himself as simply Andreas. As if he could ever be just that. But, of course, she'd known who he was. Ariana had only laughed at his imperious command to let him or his team know if she needed anything.

Until she realized he'd been in earnest. That he meant to keep an eye on his father's ward.

Keep an eye, he had.

He would come to the café where she had worked every night, two huge tomes, and newspaper cuttings and reams of paperwork spread out on his table. Not a word, not a greeting after that first one. No chatting with any other customers. Just that dark gaze tracking her all over the café, until the early hours of morning, as if he found her endlessly fascinating. After the first day, he'd walked her home to the apartment, again with nary a word exchanged between them.

Ariana had never found herself so thoroughly captivated.

He had done that for a whole month before Ari had lost her patience and approached him.

Are you my very own watchdog, Your Highness?

She cringed, remembering how outrageous she'd been.

His reply: *You should not be drinking with strange men, Ms. Sakis.*

And then he'd followed her to the party where she'd proceeded to get drunk. Taken her home to her little apartment she'd shared with three other girls.

No more exchanges except her increasingly reckless taunts to break his self-assurance over the next month.

Until the afternoon the verdict had come out about her parents' deaths. There had been no doubt that her mother had deliberately caused the accident.

She'd taken her life and her husband's, a day after he'd struck Ariana.

She'd been mindless with grief, desperate to run away from her own life. Andreas hadn't asked her a single question that day, nor left her side. Like a shadow, he'd been at her back throughout the day and night as she'd flitted from the café to a party, from the party to a walk along the coast and then back to her apartment.

Finally, she had broken down into anguished sobs, finally, she had realized that she was now forever alone, a fate she'd wished for for so long. At her apartment, he had sat by her on the couch—not even their shadows touching, always so careful to not touch her even by accident—and he had started talking, uncaring of whether she was listening.

In that deep, gravelly voice of his that had been just a tether to hold on to at first.

He'd started with the reason for his stay in the little village, a question she'd asked of him countless times. Told her of how his trail had led him there.

It was the first time she'd heard of the story of the dragon and the warriors. For hours, he'd told her of his fascination with the history of Drakon and its centuries-old lore since he'd been a little boy. Of the painstaking years of research he'd put together in his free time, which was far too little and rare. Of his fierce determination to pin down the real truth behind the war the warriors had waged on the dragon.

And in the passion in his words that had been a revelation—when she'd relentlessly taunted him for being an uptight, dutiful, one-dimensional prince puffed up with his own privilege and power—Ariana had seen the man beneath the Crown Prince's mantle. A historian, a weaver of words, a dreamer; a man that struggled to survive within the constraints of his birth and his position of power without even knowing it. A man who liked her, her company, her laughter, yet wouldn't, or couldn't put it in a simple sentence.

A man who could have the world at his feet and yet saw something worthwhile in her.

The realization that somehow the Crown Prince of Drakon, powerful and gorgeous, needed her just as much as she needed him, had reverberated through her.

As dawn had painted the sky a myriad of purples and pinks, his voice had slowly guided Ariana back to the world, to the life waiting for her.

Through her death, her mother had given her a gift. She had given Ariana her own life back.

With a fiercely alive feeling coursing through her veins, she had done what she'd been dying, but had been terrified, to do, until then. She had wiped her tears away roughly, kneeled between his long legs and pressed her mouth to his.

Her first kiss, she had decided so full of herself, would be the Crown Prince's.

Of course, he hadn't kissed her back as she'd mashed her lips against his. Tenderly, he'd clasped her jaw and pushed her back while she'd been burning with humiliation and thwarted desire, had guided her to her room, tucked her in, waited until she fell into a dreamless sleep.

The next morning, she'd woken up, brimming with a renewed verve for life and determined to have him, in whatever form she could.

Thee mou, she'd been playing with fire. Was it any wonder she'd been burned?

He'd made her feel so secure that night—a feeling she'd never known. Like she could survive the bitterest grief if only she had his words, *him* by her side.

Except she hadn't foreseen that what had attracted him to her would be what he would despise in the end.

"Challenging everything I had ever believed in," Andreas said, pulling her back into the now, a strange glitter in those dark eyes, "about myself, about the world, about my place in the world.

"You were this skinny, reckless seventeen-year-old and the first person I had ever met in my life who…"

"Who what?" she whispered, desperate for more. Even knowing that this self-indulgence would only lead to pain.

"Who didn't care how powerful, educated, or accomplished I was. With you, I was…" she'd never seen him lost for words, yet right then, she was sure he was choosing them carefully "…just Andreas for the first time."

They were words Ariana had never heard him say before. Almost regretful. A little wistful. They gouged open a longing she'd shut away.

Tears filled her throat. She wanted to pound at him for never saying those things to her then, for never telling her… No. Ruthlessly, she pulled herself to the present. They would have never survived, she needed to hold on to that.

He slowly disentangled himself from her, pushed away a lock of hair that had fallen onto her jaw. Small touches. Calculated touches. Her skin prickled. "I will make you a promise, Ari."

She scowled, more angry with herself than with him. "It won't be without some hidden motive."

And this time, he really smiled. The flash of his even white teeth against his darkly olive skin was breathtaking.

Unlike him, patience had never been her strong suit. "What is it, your promise?"

"I will not touch you until you come to me. I will not take you, *agape mou*, until you beg me to take you. Until you crawl into my bed and ask me to be inside you.

"Taking you when you can't breathe for wanting me…it is unlike any high I've known."

Ariana jerked away from him, slumberous warmth pooling low in her belly. A throbbing between her legs. "Like I did the last time."

A flare of heat darkened those impossible black eyes. It was all there in them—the log cabin at the foot of the mountains, the storm that had been raging outside for a week, the huge king bed with soft-as-sin sheets and Andreas and she stuck inside, with their supplies dwindling every day and the fire between them raging higher with every moment.

The knowledge that she had turned eighteen four weeks earlier was explosive in that silent cabin; that they had both been ignoring King Theos's summons; the knowledge that her dare in trapping the Crown Prince, who seemed to be made of stone and rock like the mountains around them, far too dangerous when she'd seen the evidence of his attraction to her finally in those first few days in the cabin.

Until the day he had decided that he was going to give in.

Sparks filled her body at the memory of that decadent night. It was the night she had begun to understand the uptight, arrogant Crown Prince, to realize what she'd thrown herself into. But it had been too late.

She'd already fallen in love with him.

Her fingers shaking to hold the duvet, Ariana pushed out the breath lodged in her chest. Barely a few hours with him and she was on fire. She cleared her hoarse throat.

"Why?"

He shrugged. "To level the field a little."

"This is exactly what you wanted when you kidnapped me—me at your mercy."

"Yes, but having you at my mercy when you have no fight in you..." he made a bored sound "...that is not the Ariana I want. What fun is tormenting you when you have no say in it?

"This way, I will know that when I'm inside you this time, you have surrendered despite the little self-preservation it seems you have developed."

Thee mou, it was impossible. The man she had married would have never been open to a challenge like that, much less taunt her with it. He would have never given the reins of anything to her hands. Much less his revenge scheme. Or the simple matter of when they'd have sex.

Had he changed or was it just a game?

He leaned a hip against the wall, all lean masculinity and hungry eyes. "Since you've always blamed me for wanting to control everything, I will leave this in your hands. We will have sex only when you want it."

"Don't you get it? I'm not self-destructive anymore, Andreas. The last time burned me enough for an entire lifetime."

Sudden stillness seemed to come over him. His gaze probed hers, as if he wanted to plumb the depths of her. "Did I burn you, Ariana?"

The question was not a taunt or even a rebuke. It

rang with curiosity that made her stomach twist. Tears pricked behind her eyelids, making him a shimmery vision.

Say no, Ari. Let the guilt be your own.

"Yes," she whispered. "I still have scars from it."

He nodded, a thoughtful look shuttering away his thoughts. "Then I owe you this, *ne*? This little game of ours can proceed as you want it or it could end as soon as you desire."

She trusted this reasonable Andreas even less than the controlling one. "End?"

"You could get naked and invite me to join you in the bed right now." Their gazes flicked to the bed and back. The soft duvet seemed to burn her skin. "I could give you the wedding night you'd have had tonight with your adorable little fiancé." His eyes hardened to dark chips, his mouth edging into that cruelly ruthless curve. "The longer you hold me off, the longer this whole thing will take."

The bastard! He had nicely trapped her. She was damned to stay with him the longer she denied this thing between them, and she was damned if she gave in. Because it had been apparent within two minutes of seeing him again, within seconds of breathing that scent of him, that she was into the special brand of masculinity that was only Andreas Drakos.

"You will be waiting a long time, Andreas. And we both know being denied what you want is a foreign concept you, *ne*?

"Also, from what I remember, celibacy makes you extra cranky."

"True, but after dealing with your deceit, my tolerance for everything has changed, Ari. You have no idea what or who I've become anymore." He turned and left the room, closing the door behind him.

Ariana buried her face in her hands, panicking over the lack of panic. Did she believe him? Would he truly give her a choice now that he had her close? And even if she did somehow resist not falling into the old patterns, she scoffed at herself, what was the point if it meant being his wife again?

A groan erupted from her mouth.

He was right in one thing, though.

Just because he had her where he wanted didn't mean she was going to roll over and let him do as he pleased. The image that her overactive mind supplied at that made the rub of her thighs excruciating.

This time, she knew what came of playing with fire. What came of tangling with Andreas Drakos.

First things first, she needed to take a shower, wash off the grime and doubts from the day she'd had so far. Ari made a note to thank the stewardess for the new set of underwear and designer jeans with their tags still intact, all in several sizes. Several shirts and blouses, too.

Why Andreas's private jet had a supply of women's underwear and clothes was something she was not going to dwell on. Not her business.

Shedding her underwear with a grimace, she grabbed a towel and walked into the small, but luxuriously decadent shower.

The jet head of steaming hot water on her tense muscles was glorious. She scrunched her nose at the row of high-end perfumed shampoos and gels, and found a bar of soap with minimum ingredients.

Running away was not an option. Avoiding him was

not an option. Staying married to a man who thrived on control like it was air—even without the history between them—was not an option.

Being the Queen of Drakon…a hysterical laugh hurtled past her throat, was not at all an option.

Her only option, she stilled with her hands in her hair, was the truth. Andreas would not let her go until he figured out why she'd deceived him, until he understood how any woman, much less Ari, could walk away from him.

But the truth was a jagged, thorny, twisted mass. Her hand moved to the scar on her lower belly.

There were other things she could make him see. She could convince him, for one thing, that it hadn't been a juvenile game to her. That she had been foolish, naive, not willfully destructive. That leaving him had been a point of survival.

She had to convince him that she could never be that Ari again. That she would never put him or his precious Drakon or his duties to the Crown before her life. That she would never love him, never put her obsession for him before her happiness.

That she had learned how destructive love could be.

CHAPTER FOUR

I STILL HAVE SCARS.

What had he done to hurt her so much?

Andreas had hated her for two years, had dreamed of ways he would ruin her when he got his hands on her.

And now that he had her…now that he had found her on the eve of her wedding to another man, the rage and betrayal simmered down, morphed into something much more insidious.

All his energy in the last hour had gone into burying the urge to stalk back into the rear cabin and demand what the hell she had meant by it.

The sight of her—the globes of her breasts falling up and down, the expanse of golden flesh, the pulse beating violently at her neck, the defiant tilt of her chin… No, right now, he wanted her more than he wanted answers. His fingers itched to run through the silky mass of her hair, to reach that sensitive spot above the nape of her neck and see if she'd respond with a moan.

He could have spanned that tiny waist with his hand, brought her up to him until those breasts crushed against his chest, could have kissed away the dare in her eyes. Within seconds, he could have had her panting for him.

Could have pressed her down onto that bed, torn out her underwear and buried himself inside her. The images his thoughts painted made him shift uncomfortably in his seat.

Thee mou, that's all he needed, to give his staff a view of his inconvenient arousal. But instead of satisfying his body's craving, he'd made that ridiculous promise desperate to banish those shadows from her eyes.

There had been something so fragile about her in that moment. As if a single wrong word about the pills could forever shatter her.

Damn his arrogance for forgetting that anything that involved Ariana could never be simple.

"Your Highness? Andreas?" Petra repeated, a little impatience slipping into her tone.

He met her silent accusation and shrugged apologetically. He could hardly blame her. After all, he'd heard nothing of what she'd said in the past fifteen minutes. Tilting his head up, he found Ariana.

Tension filled his shoulders and neck.

A white dress shirt, custom made for him, hung loose on her slender frame and was tucked into a pair of tight jeans that seemed to have been poured onto her lithe body.

The denim hugged the long muscles of her thighs and the flare of her hips. A moment's relief filled him. She did not look as unhealthy as he'd assumed earlier. Her wavy hair, she had tied into a messy knot at the back of her head. A knot he had reveled in undoing, as many times as he'd wanted.

She wore no jewelry except for a thin gold chain.

Her gaze flicked to each member of his team, an array of expressions passing through her face. When she saw Petra, a little frown appeared between her brows. When she saw Thomas, one of his oldest security guards, she threw herself at him with a grin.

A grin that turned her from that wary, resentful woman he'd kidnapped to that smiling girl he'd known long ago. Not that it was news that Ariana had always found more in common with the staff than him.

And then her eyes found him. With a regal nod that would have made the starchiest of his royal ancestors proud, she took a seat on the opposite side of the cabin. When the steward inquired if she wanted to eat, she rattled off food enough for his entire team.

All vegetarian, he remembered. At least, his private chef was more equipped than Andreas himself had been to feed her.

Andreas continued to listen to his team's updates with one ear while he watched her polish off most of the food she'd ordered. A little color returned to her cheeks and her hair glittered like drying copper left out in the sun for too long as it began falling from her knot.

He went back to discussing the security arrangements for the upcoming coronation, the details of the new trade deal he would be signing with their neighbor courtesy of Nikandros and Gabriel. "Petra?" He was about to ask her to bring him the proposal the Crown Council wanted him to push to the cabinet when he saw Ariana standing before him.

"Do you intend to work the entire flight?"

He lowered his head back to his work. "Yes. My

coronation is in two months and I have let my duties slide in the last few months. Nikandros has been carrying the brunt of them."

She sat down in front of him, and raised her brows when he silently stared at her. Her skin had that freshly scrubbed look. Her body, lithe and toned, he fought the urge to give in.

"You…ditched work? Had hell frozen over?"

He frowned, remembering the number of times after they had returned to Drakon that she had pled with him to take the day off. Or to spend the evening with her. Or at the least, to eat dinner with her every day.

And he remembered his answers very well, too.

No.

He'd always said no, pushed her every request off as juvenile or attention-seeking. He'd been far too busy trying to prove to his father that his lapse in judgment was limited to marrying her. That he was still capable of representing Drakon at the oil summit that year. That he could shoulder the tremendous task of digging Drakon out of the financial pit it had fallen into.

And then one day, she…had stopped asking.

How hadn't he noticed that until now?

"I had other things on my mind."

She flicked her gaze to his face and then back to her hands on the table. "I'm sure losing your father must have been very hard."

He laughed. Maybe he could tell her how terrified Theos had been that Andreas would kill him with his bare hands. That would discourage the sympathy in her eyes. "I was obsessed with finding you."

"Oh."

Petra stood silently by them. Waiting for him to dismiss Ariana, he slowly realized. It was not an incorrect presumption. Nor out of place.

Andreas did not let work slide for anyone. Even when he'd been searching for Ariana the last year, Petra had accompanied him most of the time. He'd done as much as he could to stop Nik from drowning under the weight of Drakon. Petra had been with him since he'd returned from the navy at eighteen and his father had chosen her to be his secretary. She knew him, knew his priorities. Maybe even came closest to a friend, though the simple art of making friends had never been allowed to him.

Petra knew him enough to come to the conclusion that whatever he was doing with Ariana, which bordered on the insane, would not affect his other functions.

The words to dismiss Ariana hovered over his lips when he noticed the edge in her smile, the whiteness of her knuckles gripping the table.

"Petra, we will continue later."

Petra hovered, her shock clear in the air. Andreas frowned and let her see it. *Christos*, his entire team had been with him for too long if Petra was questioning his orders.

Ariana crossed her legs in a casual gesture but the tension didn't leave her mouth. The flash of vulnerability reminded him again of how young she'd been then.

The cabin was now mostly empty for his look had dispersed his team. He let the silence build.

She had come with an agenda.

He waited patiently. And with a thrum of anticipation. She had always been full of crazy schemes. Like when she'd suggested they run away to the States for a couple of years and leave Drakon behind. When he had looked astonished at that, she'd modified it to say she'd wanted to backpack through Europe for a couple of months while he sorted out Drakon and its myriad problems, since their marriage hadn't been publicized.

The thought of reckless Ariana wandering through the hostels in Europe while he stayed back in Drakon... he had shot her down quite harshly.

Only now, however, he began to see the pattern. Crazy or not, he had denied her everything she had asked for. He'd given her over to his father, returning to the apartment when he'd needed sex. When he couldn't go without touching her for another minute. When he'd made some headway through the myriad of issues on his desk and she was his reward for it.

As if he'd ration his quota of her.

And every time he'd gone to see her, he'd found her to be increasingly restless, coming up with crazier plans.

He had given her the most coveted role in his life, in all of Drakon and it had been utterly lost on Ariana.

How had he forgotten those months of their marriage? It had been hell, the direct contrast of the months they'd spent in the village.

"Did you ever sleep with her?"

His head jerked up at her soft whisper.

The filthy curse that had been about to fly from his mouth arrested when he saw that her question was in earnest. The wariness in her expression, as if she were bracing for the answer, the way she seemed to retreat into herself... It galled him that even when she was in the wrong, Ariana made the most primal, possessive, protective urges come out in him.

"You lost the right to ask me that." But her question rankled. "Are you asking me if I cheated on you when we were together?"

"No." Her immediate denial seemed to surprise her just as much as it did him. "I don't think so."

He leaned back and wrapped his arm around the seat. Wanting to touch her became secondary to the questions building up in his head. "I'm beginning to realize you did not think much of me when we were together."

"No. I thought the world of you, actually," she replied in that honest way she used to have. So where had it all gone wrong? "I knew..." Her gaze was serious when she met his. "I know that you wouldn't have cheated on me.

"I meant before...before we met. Or maybe after." She sighed. "But like you said, I've no right to ask that question."

Just as easily as she provoked his ire, she mollified it. "Petra is my employee. A woman who depends on me for her livelihood. You're aware that my sister, Eleni, was born of an affair between Theos and my nanny. Do you think anything could provoke me into repeating his scandalous, abusive behavior?"

Ariana looked away. There could be a hundred women ready to fall at his feet among his employees like Petra, a hundred more who adored the very ground their Crown Prince walked on. He didn't notice the women as anything but staff members.

Petra was no more than his three aides, who were thankfully all men, no more than his security guard

Thomas, no more than his tailor, or his fitness instructor or his chef.

Another cog in the complex machinery that made his life run smoothly.

And yet... "You worshipped your father."

From the moment they had returned to the capital city, Ariana had seen the frightening truth. The man she had married was really no different from the cold, ruthless King Theos who had looked at her just as her father had done—as if she were a failure. A stain that had to be hidden far away from the gilded brightness of his palace.

"There were days when you were frighteningly similar to him." As if the world and the people in it were accessories to his own life. They were present only to provide his life with certain value.

Even Ariana had been another cog, just a pleasurable one.

His self-imposed isolation at the village, she'd made the mistake of thinking that was his life. Instead it had been a stolen pocket of time.

He laid his head back now and rubbed his jaw with the base of his palm. A bristly stubble had come in since this afternoon. Coupled with the dark shadows under his eyes, he looked a mess. Tired and almost imperfect.

A twinge of ache settled in Ari's chest. It was that same ferocious protectiveness for a man who owned the world, who didn't need it that had led her into following him into fire. Had she gained no sense in ten years?

"Because at the height of his regime my father had

been a magnificent statesman. Nik had a better measure of him far before I did. He hated that Theos alienated him from me." The regret in his words stunned Ariana. "All I saw in Theos was the man who equipped me to rule Drakon. A man who'd worked tirelessly for years to make me perfect. A man who only wanted me to have the world and rule it.

"Only later did I realize that in his personal life, Theos was a manipulative monster."

Ariana bit her lip. She didn't have much time. Not if she wanted to stop him from parading her next to him come coronation day in front of all of Drakon. "I would have given anything for you to see that side of King Theos back then, Andreas."

"It must be so tempting to put this all on him, but he only aided you, Ariana."

She caught his hands on the table and laced her fingers through his. To anchor him to her, to not lose him to the memory of a cruel old man. "That's not true. He knew everything that was going on between us. Every fight, every disagreement. Petra relayed everything to him."

"He was a ruthless bastard, yes, but do not put your faults on him."

When he jerked his hand away, she held fast. For a man who spent hours at his desk signing treaties, he'd always had such rough hands.

"Andreas, it was never my idea to fake… I never agreed to pretend that I was dead. I only signed the papers dissolving our marriage. I took the money your father offered, yes, but I…"

He pulled his hand away from her as if she was poison.

Ariana stood up and blocked him. "If you're determined to make us walk through this hell again, at least listen to my side."

His hands fisted. "How did you realize what he had done if you didn't even look back?"

"I received all the paperwork through a lawyer. God, I didn't even completely understand the ramifications for a month. I panicked and called Giannis who told me what Theos had done behind my back."

Such bleak rage emanated in his black eyes that Ariana stepped back. "Of course, you kept in touch with your little security guard friend."

The insinuation in his tone cut bone deep. "Giannis was my friend. He understood what I was going through. He…"

"What happened when Giannis told you of Theos's convoluted lies? Why didn't you call me then?"

"It was too late."

"Too late to tell me that you were alive?"

"Your engagement had been announced. I was not in a good—"

"What, Ari?" His voice caught, his words clipped like hard gravel. "You thought I deserved to continue believing that my young wife was dead. Probably at my own father's hands or because of my own negligence, of which you'd been complaining for months."

"You thought he killed me?"

"Yes." The haunted look she'd thought she'd imagined was back in his eyes. The pain there…it was a knife in her chest. "He didn't hide his satisfaction that you were out of my life for good. After all his rages for weeks because I had ruined our legacy—because

I had…" He ran a hand through his hair roughly. "It was the first time I saw Theos for what he could be.

"But it was only a suspicion. I threw myself into my work, I alienated Nik, I hurt Eleni. I thought I was going mad, suspecting my own father of a terrible thing.

"Theos hated the thought of you as my wife. It was as much a shock to him as it was to me that I…married you. That I could make such an unprecedented, uncharacteristic decision with my life."

"Then why did you, Andreas?" The question burst from her lips. A question she should have asked instead of running away. "You could have had me for as long as you wanted and walked away. I wouldn't have made a peep."

"I told you. You were a virgin that night and I didn't use protection."

"We could have waited to see if there were any consequences."

"I seduced you!"

"You took me to bed after I threw myself at you for months. Repeatedly."

"Still, you were eighteen, my father's neglected ward. You had no one in the world to look after your interests. What I did was—"

"Don't you dare take that away from me. I wanted you, God, I needed you just as much you needed me that night.

"But after, you…could have walked away. You could have paid me off. You could have… Why marry the shallow, ditzy, reckless failure that I was? Why marry me when you knew what your real life was like, when you knew how wrong I was for you?"

His breath was rough, his eyes blazing with an unholy light. "Because I got used to it."

Her heart thumped so hard against her rib cage, Ari could hardly breathe. "Used to what?"

"Used to being adored by you. Used to being loved by you." Shoulders tense, he rubbed his nape. For a man who exuded arrogant self-confidence out of every pore, the gesture was disconcertingly hesitant. "I was the center of your universe and it made me lose sight of who I was and who you were.

"Thanks to Theos, I had tasted every kind of power that was to be had in the world. But you, Ariana…your adoration for me even as you mocked everything I was in this world, it was a drug I couldn't give up on.

"I thought I could keep that, keep you for myself. One selfish indulgence that I would allow myself.

"It was the biggest mistake of my life. In that, Theos was right."

Ariana wound her arms around her trembling body, something deflating out of her. Hope, after all this time. Hope that he would admit that he'd married her because he'd loved her, too. That he had been shattered at the loss of her not because he felt responsible or guilty but something else.

"Then put a stop to that mistake. Don't continue the farce of our marriage."

"What do you suggest? That I marry another woman, make her my Queen and keep you on the side?

"Should I give you the place you're so determined to prove is yours, Ari? Should I visit you in the dark as if you were a paid whore, a kept mistress my father encouraged me to make of you?

"Would you have me become the monster Theos and you made me out to be? Because nothing has changed, *pethi mou*. I still want you with that same madness.

"You're still a weakness—the only one that I can't overcome."

Her hands boldly reached for his face, the scent of her skin a familiar twining in his blood.

With his fingers on her wrist, he stayed her movements. He could not bear to be touched by her. Not yet, and not like this. Not when he felt like a cauldron of volatile emotions, not when all he wanted was to push her into the bed, and bury himself in her.

"I shouldn't have run away like that, not with his help. But…but it was not a bid for freedom because I got bored with you or because I was shallow enough to fall in love with another man who was nothing but my friend. It was not a fickle game."

"No?"

"No. I…loved you. You. But loving you… I realized, slowly began to kill me and in the end, I chose survival."

Her words pinged through his mind like a bullet ricocheting through a closed room. Puncturing and tearing, scraping and scorching the walls of his mind.

He wanted to hate her as he had done for two years. He'd opened the Pandora's box of their relationship willingly and it seemed there was no end to the things that could come crawling out.

Things Andreas wasn't sure he wanted to face.

"How was I killing you?"

Utter helplessness filled her face. And it was seeing

that in her eyes, when Ariana never stopped fighting, that made him believe everything she'd said.

"It doesn't matter anymore," she whispered.

The pilot broke the tense silence with an update that they were landing soon.

Between mourning her death for eight years and the discovery of her treachery, he had forgotten that he was at the root of this.

The enormity of his marrying Ariana had only sunk through when his father had confronted him. Had shown him the hopeless state of the treasury of Drakon, the mounting national debt. The alliance that Theos had carefully cultivated with Gabriel Marquez, to make his sister the Queen of Drakon, crumbling to dust.

So he'd immediately tried to right his world.

He'd been prepared to do anything for Drakon but not give her up. She was only a small part of his life, he'd told his father. After all, the Queen's role was only titular in Drakon.

For the first month, it had worked. She became his escape from the weight of his nation's problems. From his father's spiraling moods and sudden rages. Then slowly, things had changed.

It was as if he'd lived in two different realities, one as the Crown Prince and one as the man obsessed with his young wife.

As long as they didn't merge, he'd convinced himself his world would be all right.

As long as he didn't let her take over his life, as long as she meant nothing more to him than physical relief at the end of a hard day, a pleasure he looked forward to at night, as long as he didn't let her disrupt his duties ever again... *Thee mou*, he'd made so many promises to Theos just to keep her.

I chose survival.

Like a bone-deep bruise, those words lingered.

Was he prepared to face what he'd done to make his bright, cheerful, eighteen-year-old wife flee the moment his back had been turned, to learn that he was the one responsible for putting those shadows in Ari's eyes?

Suddenly, he questioned the sanity of everything he'd been doing since he'd found she was alive.

CHAPTER FIVE

MILES OF NEATLY manicured land greeted Ariana as the jet taxied into the private airstrip and they disembarked. The same airstrip where King Theos's staff had seen her into a jet that left Drakon ten years ago.

It wasn't as bitterly cold as it had been in Colorado. But the air was just as crisp and fresh. In the distance, the outline of the mountain range made the perfect horizon. Tall palm trees dotted a neat perimeter around the airstrip.

As Ari stood there, a strange thread of homecoming rang through her. She hadn't thought she'd missed Drakon but she had. Or maybe it was the sense of purpose that she'd found in herself that changed her view.

She wasn't swinging from guilt over her mother's death to the sudden, terrifying taste of freedom. Not running away from the fear that maybe her father had been right and she was good for nothing.

Suddenly, she was glad she was here. If only she could throw every derogatory word her father had called her about being a failure in his face, if only her mother were here to see that Ari had made something of herself, that Ari was utterly happy...

But you've not been utterly happy. Focused, dedi-

cated, busy to the point of exhaustion and restless. But not happy, never happy.

That girl who'd laughed recklessly, who'd loved so generously, she'd just stifled her, desperate to avoid that heartbreak again. As if to punish herself for losing her baby boy.

But had it been anything more than a half-life?

Had it been anything but penance?

Three bulletproof cars arrived on the curb, the black-and-gold flags whipping in the wind. Three separate teams waited for Andreas's attention, their curiosity evident in their scrutiny of her.

Her every action was going to be scrutinized and sanitized, her every word dissected to ensure it measured up against Andreas's image. But no one was going to intimidate her this time.

Andreas stood before her, his eyes holding hers captive.

She shivered and was immediately covered in a warm, long coat that fell past her knees.

Sandalwood and his body heat combined to make a potent drug emanating from the thick wool. The familiarly comforting scent curled through her.

His hand around her shoulders caught them up in their own little world. So close, she could see the tiny golden flecks in his eyes. Feel the wiry strength of his lean body.

She stood mutely as he settled the coat around her shoulders and buttoned up the first couple buttons so that her chest was adequately protected.

Her heart thudded when he lifted the ring finger of her left hand. The tiny point-one-carat diamond struggled to throw off even a spark. With gentle movements that suggested he loathed putting her through any discomfort, a startling contrast as he ripped the fabric of her very life apart, he pulled the ring off her finger.

His jet-black gaze held hers in a possessive dare as he threw the ring into the acreage behind them.

Ariana jerked but his hand around her nape arrested her. Even for her five-nine height, he had to bend down. "Welcome home, Ariana," he said, in a silky voice at her ear, before touching his mouth to the corner of hers.

His lips were warm against her skin, sending pockets of heat through her. Her entire body trembled at the searing contact, her hands rising to his chest automatically. To hold him close, to soak in his warmth.

She let her hands fall to her sides, heat swamping her face.

Andreas would always have this power over her, this…ability to turn her inside out. Accepting that was strangely calming.

She needed closure just as much as Andreas did.

She needed to figure out if it would always be a half-life without him. And if it was, would the little Andreas was offering be enough this time?

Because there was one thing she knew.

Andreas Drakos could never love.

The drive back to the palace was long but thankfully not intimate. Three of his staff, including Petra, joined them in the expansive limo, leaving Ariana to sit opposite him.

His cuffs rolled back to reveal strong forearms. Ariana followed the column of his throat, his chest tapering to a lean waist and then to his legs stretched out.

His trousers cleanly molded the length of his muscular thighs.

Needing a reprieve from that overwhelming masculinity, Ariana leaned back and closed her eyes.

His words, assertive and rapid-fire, assaulted her senses.

Andreas answered questions and asked his own. Matters that would have been over her head and, quite honestly, boring, made more sense to Ariana this time.

Now, instead of being told by everyone how rapier-sharp Andreas's mind was, she saw it in play. His memory was astounding, his attention to detail when he was mired in so many matters awe-inspiring. She listened in fascination as he took the first draft of a speech written by one of his press team and shredded it to pieces by calling out clichéd phrases and for not addressing any of the scare rhetoric that the media had been doling out about him following Theos's madness in the last few years.

For the first time in decades, the populace was questioning what the royal house was doing for the people.

It was his coronation speech, Ariana realized, with unwise curiosity.

Absolute conviction rocked in his every gesture. "Drakon enters a new era with me at the helm. We shall not rest on the past laurels of the House of Drakos anymore. The royal house will begin the process of decoupling from the cabinet in coming years."

Ariana scoffed. The sound was like an elephant blaring in the quiet interior.

"Do you have something to say, Ariana?"

"Nothing you would want said in company, Your Highness," she replied sweetly.

"We do not want my staff to believe you're afraid of me, do we?"

That put her spine up like nothing could. Even as she'd been utterly overwhelmed by him back then, she'd never let him intimidate her. There was a distinction, an important one they both knew.

She sat forward, looking him in the eye. "Decoupling the House of Drakos and the Drakon cabinet? Andreas Drakos walking away from power to rule the lives of millions? That's like a lion giving up its ability to hunt.

"That power is in your blood, your bones, your very skin. You will never do it."

"I'm not giving up power so much as I'm redistributing it into the right hands," he said surprisingly receptive to her criticism. "I want more checks and balances. The Crown Council was supposed to do that, but Theos controlled them with his power and wealth. Until there was no one to question his executive command of the cabinet.

"Nikandros already has the economy of Drakon in his hand. He's always been the financial genius.

"Eleni, if Gabriel lets her accept my proposal, will become the formal liaison between the palace and the hundreds of charities we support."

"Your brother and sister? That's your power distribution—other members of the House of Drakos? You think they will go against your wishes?"

"You would understand if you had…" He bit his accusation off, aware of the staff watching them with a hungry fascination. "My father hoarded power, until it drove him to madness. Until he began to think of even me as his enemy.

"I don't intend to let that happen to me.

"After all, I have a personal life now and I intend to enjoy it."

As much as she wanted to fight it, the truth of it shone in his eyes. "Control is everything to you."

In the intimacy of the dark night, even as he had shocked her with his demands and his carnality, he'd not once let her lead. Even as he'd lost himself in the pleasures of sex, it had still been very much calculated.

The very devil glinted in his eyes. "Is that another challenge then, *agapita*?"

She felt a collective hiss of exhale from the two women in the car. Not that she could blame them.

He's mine, she wanted to say, that wildness she'd tried to bury surfacing with a vengeance. Maybe it was the air of her homeland, maybe it was facing Andreas as the woman she was now, but restlessness slithered under her skin.

"Don't make promises—" she raised a brow, and almost pulled it off "—that you cannot keep, Your Highness."

His eyes shone with unholy mirth, deep grooves dug into his cheeks. His brows went all off-kilter. "Worried that you might not be able to resist me after all?"

A reluctant smile curved her lips and she looked out the window.

The outline of the mountain range became vague as the car entered the city, the white stone structure of the King's Palace sitting atop the small hill emerging ahead.

Was he serious about all these changes? What had brought it on?

The more she spent time with him, the more she

was realizing that something had changed in him. But the very idea of revealing the last bit of truth she had hidden, the condemnation in his eyes if he learned of what she had lost... Fear skated over her spine.

They arrived at the King's Palace with very little fanfare.

The lack of his family's presence was conspicuous and Ariana was caught between relief and a bit of disappointment, if she were honest.

She had obsessively followed every bit of palace gossip over the last few years. The changes it seemed Andreas was determined to bring to Drakon. Even the rising sentiment against the once-beloved Crown Prince.

She knew that the Daredevil Prince, Nikandros, had returned to Drakon after a years-long rift between him and Andreas. That Nikandros had married the ex-soccer player Mia Rodriguez and had two infant children.

That Eleni Drakos, dubbed with the cheap moniker the Plain Princess of Drakon for years, had recently married Gabriel Marquez—Isabella Marquez's brother, the same woman Andreas had been engaged to after Ariana fled.

Were these changes Andreas had brought out too?

Two security guards accompanied her through the miles of corridors.

Barely a staff of five, Andreas's personal retinue greeted them. She was shown into a set of rooms done in elegant creams and mauves. A lounge, a bathroom that spanned the square footage of her legal aid agency, and a massive bed that was the pride of place in the bedroom.

"Do not even think of running, Ari," Andreas suddenly whispered at her ear and Ariana jerked.

Her hand fluttered to his chest and she kept it there now, loving the solid feel of him under it. Needing suddenly the reassurance of his presence before he was lost to her in the maze of the palace.

"Do not give me reason to, Your Highness," she quipped back, trying to hide her elation that he hadn't forgotten about her as soon as they had set foot in the palace. That, this time, he had actually brought her to the palace and not hidden her away.

God, but she was pathetic that even the smallest crumbs from him made her heart dance.

He didn't smile. But covered her hand with his, the long fingers tangling with hers. "Rest up for a couple of hours." His gaze caressed her face, as if looking for proof that she wouldn't faint again. "My family wishes to meet you."

"More people who hate me, yay," she said, a sudden panic seizing her chest. "Andreas, couldn't we—"

"No, Ariana. I have defied every tenet I had for my personal life and pushed every Crown Council member that hates me to the edge by bringing you here." A dark smile touched his eyes. "You're ten years late, *pethi mou*. Drakon wants its queen and I want my wife."

Ariana watched him leave, but instead of fear, a fierce determination filled her.

She had gone from a train wreck to something hopefully akin to a woman who knew her own mind.

Was it possible for the Crown Prince of Drakon to change, too?

CHAPTER SIX

"WELL, IS SHE HERE? What does she do? Where did she go after she left you?" Eleni demanded the moment Andreas walked into the Green Room at King's Palace.

His head was pounding after the quick report he'd had from his aides.

Nikandros had been right. The situation with his popularity ratings was much worse than even he'd anticipated.

Soon, he had to find a way to turn the sentiment that was rising against him. "Calm down, Eleni," Gabriel muttered. Andreas felt a flash of sympathy for his brother-in-law. It had to be hard to see Eleni continue like the little dynamo she was when she was pregnant.

"She's a lawyer," Andreas answered while accepting the drink Nik had poured him. "She set up a legal aid agency with the money she took from Father."

Gabriel whistled, a devilish light in his green eyes. "The controlling bastard that you are, I always thought you needed a woman with steel balls. A woman who could perhaps be your saving grace. She sounds like it."

"I didn't realize I needed saving."

The insufferable smile slid from Gabriel's mouth. "You do. Before you end up like your father."

Nothing fractured his self-control these days more than being compared to Theos. "I interfered in Eleni's life because I wanted her to be happy. Because I knew what Theos did to her and I wanted to do right by her."

"Leave it, Gabriel. It is his life," said Nik.

"Being a member of the illustrious House of Drakos doesn't mean you're above the law," Mia added, glaring at Nik.

"She gave him little choice when she decided to marry another man, Mia." Eleni's loyalty for her brothers had always been absolute. The scowl on Gabriel's face made Andreas grin despite the open bashing of his morals. "If it came out later that the King of Drakon's secret first wife had committed bigamy, it would—"

"It would have made the scandal of the century for the populace of Drakon," said that husky voice Andreas would know in the darkest of nights.

Ariana walked into the evening lounge where they had all gathered for predinner drinks with the aplomb of a queen. Every cell in him came to attention, his skin tight over his muscles. There was a bright glitter in her eyes.

"A headline that could rival even the stories about that first band of warriors conquering the dragon. And believe me, your people need new material. That dragon lore..." Ariana rolled her eyes when Eleni, a staunch believer in all myths, dragons and the superiority of the House of Drakos, gasped. "It gets boring as hell after a while. Not to mention, it isn't something to crow about to the world."

Stunned silence met her prosaic announcement.

Disbelief etched on his family's faces. Andreas flexed his fingers trying to forget the feel of her silky skin.

"Andreas," she said, "introduce your family. After all, I did answer your royal summons." She turned to the rest of them and smiled. "Apparently, ten years has only made Andreas's penchant for control worse."

Nikandros broke the ice. "We didn't give him a choice, Ms. Sakis." He took her hand in his and shook it. "Welcome to Drakon, I'm—"

"The Daredevil Prince," she said with that wide smile of hers. Andreas scowled. She leaned into Nik, her voice lowered to a whisper that wasn't quite one. "Come, Nikandros," she said with that easy familiarity that was second nature to her, that made Andreas want to pull her to his side, "you really don't expect me to believe that Andreas bowed to pressure from someone else, do you?"

Eleni bristled. "Is it hard to believe that we would want to meet our brother's wife?"

"As far as I remember, Andreas did not share a close relationship with you or Nikandros. I have mostly found that he is incapable of nurturing relationships."

Andreas stared into his drink, knowing that she was right. It was only in the last few years that he'd begun undoing the damage he'd done to his brother and sister.

He had still made mistakes, as Gabriel had pointed out.

"Maybe you do not," Eleni replied, sending Ariana a cool look, "know our brother as well as you think you do."

Her nostrils flared, her chin set in stubborn lines,

Ariana looked like she wanted to argue. In the end, she shrugged.

"Point to the House of Drakos," she added, with a wink at Gabriel.

Gabriel took her outstretched hand into his while Mia walked over to Ariana's side and introduced herself.

Within minutes, Ariana had Mia and Gabriel roaring with laughter. Brows raised, Nik conveyed his own surprise about her with a twitching mouth.

Irate at his brother's humor, Andreas turned to watch her. Acknowledged the fact that physical possession of Ariana was never going to be enough.

The cap-sleeved floral knee-length dress in white and pink with a string of pearls jarred with the elegant ambience of the palace as he accompanied Ariana to dinner. Her hair was in a riotous knot at the back of her head, wavy tendrils already falling away from it and framing her gamine face. Bright red lipstick made her full-lipped mouth stand out even more than usual amidst her stark features.

Even for a man who rarely understood fashion, Andreas was immediately aware that the whole outfit and makeup and what he knew of Ariana just didn't gel.

When she moved to the other end, he forced her to sit on his right. Forced her to brush her body against his as she sat down. Still, she wouldn't spare him a look.

Nothing however could leave Ariana daunted for too long. The moment the first course was served, she said, "I know what you must all be thinking. Not only is she an almost bigamist, but she has the most atrocious sense of style, *ne*?"

Mia just stared back with a rueful glint in her eye while Eleni flushed.

"You see, Andreas's secretary—who very efficiently arranged these clothes for me because your brother kidnapped me in my torn wedding dress—and I have this cold war thing going on. From years back.

"Petra is making a point that everyone loyal to Andreas is dying to make right now. That I'm not fit to polish your brother's handmade Italian boots much less to be his wife. A fact that was drilled into me with a sledgehammer in Version One of our marriage."

"By our father," Nik finished for her.

She shrugged. "In your father's defense, King Theos already knew from my father what a failure I was. I got thrown out of three finishing schools, ran away from home three times, embarrassed and humiliated my father in a hundred different ways.

"For a military general whose sparkling reputation and pride were most important, I was a huge letdown. I had neither academic smarts, nor did I fit well with his friends' high-achieving children.

"I was an utter failure, a fact he constantly reminded me of."

Andreas stilled with his glass of water halfway to his mouth. The thought of Ariana running away sat like a boulder on his chest. *Christos*, he'd never known. He'd never even asked her about her life with her parents. "Why did you run away?"

"Whenever I… I defied him, my father locked me in my room." A vacant expression emanated in her eyes. "Probably not a huge thing. But he would cut me off completely for days. I would be given food and water. But nothing else. He thought it character-building.

"I found the silence...unbearable. All it did was make me resolute that I'd never be caught again.

"Anyway, when King Theos inherited my guardianship, I don't think he knew what to do with me.

"He sent me off to a corner of Drakon until I turned eighteen. Only a few months later, there I was, his worst nightmare.

"To find out what his dear heir had done...to see me stand at his doorstep as the future Queen..." A shiver went through her.

"Theos went ballistic," Nikandros finished for her.

Eleni asked, "What did Father do?"

For the first time since she had blown into the room like a summer storm, Ariana met his gaze. "I was installed in an apartment, away from the gilded walls of the palace, a stain to be hidden away. Theos's team put me on a diet of history lessons, etiquette lessons, posture training. I was cut off from the few friends I had. Petra and her team had nothing but contempt for me. I was not allowed to leave the apartment. I was not allowed to contact anyone for fear of leaking who I was to Andreas.

"I was in a cage again. And my jailer was the man I loved, the man I had trusted."

The clatter of his fork against the plate sounded like an explosion in the room.

Her chin tilted up boldly, taut lines carved around her mouth, she stared at him.

Nik's expression became haunted. "I'm aware of our father's routine to mold people, Ms. Sakis. His penchant to strip one of every good thing. Only Andreas could ever bear his rigorous requirements and stay standing."

He turned an accusing look toward Andreas. "Where were you when this was happening?"

"If your father thought to mold me," Ariana answered with a glittering anger in her eyes, "it was only with Andreas's encouragement. Andreas visited me when he needed—" their eyes met, and he saw the dirty truth there "—a *diversion* from his busy life," she finished and looked away.

Why the hell hadn't she told him any of this back then?

Because he hadn't been available. Because he had never even asked.

Because from the moment Andreas had realized the magnitude of his mistake in marrying her, he'd tried to limit the damage. To the crown or to himself, he didn't know to this day.

"It was for your own good," he said, trying to fight the guilt that settled on him. For the first time in his life, trying to offer justification. "You had neither the education nor the background to survive in my world. You would have been shredded to pieces.

"I had to salvage the situation. I had to make you worthy of—"

Her chin reared down, her body tense. "Worthy of you, Andreas? I never pretended to be anything but what I am."

No, she hadn't. She hadn't even wanted to marry him. Only he had seduced her into it.

This was what he had done—clipped her wings, caged her, and for Ariana, for the girl who had defied her father's abusive edicts, for the girl who had loved so freely, freedom was everything. She had loved him and he had choked the life out of her.

His father had been right. Andreas only knew destruction.

He'd wanted answers and here they were. The rest of the dinner proceeded in a strained manner, Andreas unable to contribute anything more. Unable to see past the haunted look in Ariana's eyes.

Grappling with the magnitude of the mistake he'd made in marrying her and refusing to give her up, he'd retreated from her. He had given her over to his father to be molded into whatever the hell Theos thought she should be.

All he'd wanted was to get his life back to normal. Before he'd lost sight of what and who he was, and what he was not capable of.

He had delegated her to a small part in his life. The relief from the loneliness, a respite from the increasing demands of his father, an escape from the fact that Theos's dementia had begun to manifest even back then, making him feel the burden of Drakon on his shoulders.

"The dragon lore, Ms. Sakis?" Eleni piped up just as Ariana excused herself. "A band of warriors defeated the dragon and made its treasure their own. They provided land and riches to their community. What is there to not crow about?"

Ariana's gaze pinned him. "You never told anyone what we found in that old library?"

Andreas shook his head, a savage clamor inside him at how easily she had used *we*. At the light that came on in her eyes when she spoke of those months. At the connection that seemed to have survived between them despite the destruction wrought.

She moved toward him, unconscious of her own

movements, he was sure. The weight of her brown gaze, the concern in them, pinned him. "You never finished your book?"

"No," he replied, shying away from the shock in her eyes.

"What book is this?" Nikandros asked, his gaze shifting between them.

Her fingers pulled his wrist. "You never shared it with anyone?"

Feeling as if his entire insides were being pulled up for display, Andreas stepped away from her. From the emotion ringing in her eyes. "No." When he had returned and thought her dead, the last thing on his mind had been his research. And after a few years, everything relating to that time had become far too private and precious. A part of his life—*their life*—that he wasn't willing to share with anyone.

"But it was your dream, Andreas," she whispered. The loss of it shone in her eyes, in the tremble of her lips.

Had his dream meant that much to her then? *Thee mou*, he couldn't tolerate this turmoil within. Couldn't stand the weight of his guilt bearing down upon him. Anger had been so much better.

"Andreas came to that village," she said turning toward his family, her voice pitched carefully, "because he'd found a trail to the warriors' first settlement leading back hundreds of years there. We..." She colored under his gaze. "He found a manuscript that was written in one of the old Hellenic languages. He spent weeks trying to translate it.

"You know that Andreas can read and write in eight languages, right?"

Everybody in the room looked stunned. But she had eyes for no one else. Nor he for anyone but her. "There was a price to pay for defeating the dragon so easily. In fact, that manuscript suggested the leader of that band hadn't so much defeated it as made a deal with it."

"A deal?" Eleni asked.

"The dragon demanded a price. The warrior was to sacrifice his wife to its fiery jaws and it would relinquish the treasure." Her brown eyes shone with a wet brilliance.

And suddenly Andreas realized why she was so emotional about the story. Why she looked as if she was about to break like a piece of glass.

She saw him as the head of that fierce band of warriors. The man who had so ruthlessly sacrificed his wife for duty and glory, a woman who had loved him completely.

"The warrior accepted," she finished. "And became the first King.

"He was given the name Drakos and when he married again, his family became the House of Drakos."

A long sigh left her, her body almost weaving at the spot. Finally, she lifted her gaze away from him. But the recriminations he had seen there had already latched on to him.

"There you are, Mrs. Marquez. That is why I don't think it is something to celebrate. But of course Drakonites must have their tales.

"And House of Drakos its fairy-tale reputation to live up to."

Her head held high, she left the room without looking back, leaving Andreas standing stunned.

He *had* sacrificed her, hadn't he? He had treated her as a possession to be used when he needed it, a toy he could wind up when he wanted to play.

He'd given no thought, ever, to her dreams, her fears. Even to her needs. *Christos*, he hadn't treated her any better than a staff member. Or a mistress, hired for his pleasure.

It had all been about what she could give him. About his desires and wants.

Gabriel was right. He had been, he still was, just like his father. Using people for his own means, hurting the ones closest to him. It had always been hard for him to see beyond his own needs, his privilege. To see anything that he didn't control as a weakness.

It had never been about Ariana. It had always been about what she made him feel. What she brought to his life.

Now he saw the distinction between what he had done to her versus how Nikandros had been ready to sacrifice his own happiness for Mia's. Now he understood why Gabriel had been willing to love Eleni even knowing that she might not love him.

The thought of being that vulnerable felt like needles under his skin.

Had Theos destroyed his ability to care for anyone but himself?

Was he willing to do the same to Ariana again?

Ariana left the dining salon and stumbled into another vast room. She needed to catch her breath. She needed a reprieve from everything Andreas made her feel, despite her every effort to stay rational.

Pink Carrera marble as far as she could see, clawtoothed arm chairs, velvet-upholstered chaise longues, the luxury was unprecedented, understated.

Gilded portraits looked down from the walls, witness to every event. It seemed the walls themselves were seeped with the history of the House of Drakos. And yet, she knew that Andreas had had a quiet happiness in that small village that he had not found here.

Something reverberated in her at being inside the palace. She'd been denied this the last time. Because she had been deemed unfit for its hallowed halls. Denied her rightful place by his side.

Did she want it this time? Did she want to carve a place for herself in Drakon by his side?

Turning around, she saw Andreas, leaning against the high arch, his gaze studying her intently. Hands tucked into his pockets, dark shadow outlining his jawline, he was heartbreakingly gorgeous.

And determined to keep her in his life. The little fact weaved its own web around her.

"You look… I don't know what that look is, to be precise," she heard him say as she walked around the room, checking where the myriad doors led.

She stilled, stunned that he had recognized her… confusion.

Slowly, she turned around, ready to face him. "I thought you would be furious with me."

He didn't move, just raised a brow.

"I didn't mean to…wash our dirty linen in front of everyone."

"Then why did you?"

She ran a fingertip against the arm of a huge wingback chair. "Being here…unsettled me. Seeing your family look at me with accusing eyes…disconcerted me. I was ashamed of what I did and it just came pouring out.

"I… I've never been part of a big family and if they're going to be mine, I need them to understand that what I did was cowardly but not malicious."

"I'm not angry, Ariana. At least not with you."

Her head jerked up, their gazes colliding across the vast room. Was it that simple to give his forgiveness?

He shrugged, sensing her disbelief. "My family knows what Theos made me into. You've already turned them."

Only Andreas could ever bear his rigorous requirements and stay standing.

Nikandros's flyaway remark hit her hard.

"Nik? What did he mean by it? What did your father do to you?"

"It's irrelevant, Ari."

"It is not, Andreas. Our pasts have made us this. We hurt each other…because of what was done to us. Please…let me understand, too."

His face tightened, his gaze far away. "He isolated me from everyone else. I had no friends, no playmates. I was not even allowed a pet, because my father thought it would weaken me.

"He put me through rigorous physical routines, harsh enough to chill a grown man, much less a boy of ten, because he thought I was becoming a bookworm. He thought the Crown Prince could not be all brains and no brawn.

"He made me join a military unit at fifteen because he thought it would toughen me up.

"He sought to make me invincible."

And he had, in a way.

Ariana sat in the chair, stunned, the implications whirling through her head. That's why there had always been such a wall around him. In the beginning, she had thought it was his station in life, his privilege that made him oblivious to the world.

"No wonder you thrived on the isolation in that cabin." The words fell from her mouth without conscious thought.

"I do not thrive on solitude, as much as it is all I've ever known," he offered. "For years, I had no one for company except books and tutors and my father. I had no other role in life except being the Crown Prince. Not even a son to Theos. Not a brother, not a friend.

"I rarely even heard anyone call me by my name. It was always Your Highness.

"I learned to keep myself happy with my books or go crazy.

"I was not allowed to see Nik unless they were supervised visits. Anything that was assumed could be a weakness, anything that I could depend on, I was forced to get over it.

"Then slowly as I grew older, I began to chafe at Theos's restrictions. Drakon was still everything to me but Camille, Nik's mom, made me see that I could have a life outside it, too. Then Eleni, who was always there, who never asked for anything. I began to realize how different life could have been. But it was too late by then.

"Being alone became second nature.

"It became who I was."

She felt like crying. "How did you survive it?"

"How did you survive being locked up?"

Even having known the best part of him, she had

so easily stereotyped Andreas into that uncaring role. In her naive stupidity, she had barely even tried to understand the pressure he must have faced from Theos, the duress of having to fix the gaping hole of Drakon's economy.

She had always blamed Andreas for knowing her so little. Had she been any better? But suddenly, it was as if she was seeing the true Andreas for the first time.

The man at the village, and the Crown Prince— it had always seemed like two polarizing opposites that she could never understand. She had struggled to fathom how she'd misjudged him so terribly.

He had wronged her, yes. But she had done just the same.

Suddenly, she wanted the past cleared between them. She wanted a fresh start. She walked back to him, purpose in every step. "Do you believe me? That it was never my intention to deceive you?"

His jet-black gaze held hers for what felt like an eternity. Something had changed in his perception of her, she realized now. The truth of their marriage? "Does it matter to you that I believe you?"

Frustration flared and she forgot to temper her response. "Of course it does."

Only when he smiled, a soft light in his eyes, did she realize that she had betrayed herself in the now.

What he thought of her had always mattered to her.

Still mattered, it seemed.

He traced her cheek with his knuckles. As if that small fracture in her resistance of him was a prize. As if he would give her the world if only she became that Ari again.

I got used to being loved by you.

What did that truly mean? she wondered now. For a man who'd had everything, had her love meant something? Did he want that again?

His gaze searched hers, as if he wanted to see through to her soul. "Because it alleviates your guilt?"

Her hands rose to his chest. His heart thundered under her palm. She wanted to pull away the layers of clothes, feel the silk of warm skin tightly stretched over muscle. Emotions battered at her from all sides, and only this awareness of him was constant, this heat and hardness of his body the only real thing. "No, because I…never wanted to hurt you. Because I need you to know, even after all these years."

He didn't say she hadn't hurt him, and in his silence, in the things he said without saying anything, Ariana found a world of hope. The moment stretched between them, wanting and morphing, his heart thundering away under her palm, her own beating a thousand a minute.

A moment between the past and the future.

His fingers crawled to her nape, not pressing, not moving. Just touching. His other hand moved to her hip, the tips of those long fingers reaching the jut of her hip bones.

Her entire being wanted to melt in his arms. To curl up in his heat. God, this was it. This was exactly what had been missing from her life.

What her heart and soul had desperately needed.

She had needed him to understand the truth of what she had done. But given up all hope that he would look at her like this…like she still mattered.

"Andreas? Please, you have to—"

Gently, he pushed her back until he could see into her eyes. "Yes, *pethi mou*. I believe that all you did was run away the moment I turned my back," he replied, twisting her words.

She sensed his confusion and something more in that. A loss that she hadn't stood and fought for them? She waited for him to say more, to call her a coward even. After all, she'd declared again and again that she loved him, hadn't she?

But no more came from him.

"Your father went through an elaborate scheme to make me unforgivable in your eyes. He couldn't have been worried that you would chase me. You'd have hated me too much."

Something glittered in his gaze. "Are you asking me or telling me?"

It was one of those moments that defined life. A door opening. Years of tightly suppressed hope unfurling. "I'm asking you," she whispered, hiding her face in his chest.

God, she was so tired of staying strong. Of…denying, even now, that he meant something to her, after all these years.

"I would have come after you, yes." A long sigh fell from his lips. "There's no moving forward without facing the past, is there?"

A rush of tenderness filled her. "No."

He did care. He cared that he had hurt her. He cared that he had driven her away. Too little, too late, but God, she hadn't been without culpability. She hadn't made it easy with her flights of rage and her sulks and that fear that she had fallen in love with a man so horribly wrong for her. So much a despot like her father.

"I'm sorry for what I let him do to you."

But what about what you did? she wanted to ask. *What about your incapability to love me? To see me as anything other than an obsession or a weakness. Incapable of giving me a tiny, tiny piece of your heart.*

But she wouldn't be, she *wasn't* that needy girl anymore.

She didn't need to be loved by him to know her worth. Maybe she'd even lost her own ability to love, to trust someone else with her happiness, the ability to share fully of herself.

Seeing her son's small, unmoving body had done something to her.

She had lost her ability to love and he'd given up his dream.

Sanitized and sterile, weren't they perfect for each other now? "You could have any woman in the world. Why me?"

He grinned, suddenly looking incredibly boyish. "Is this one of the reasons then? That I didn't compliment you enough?"

"Compliment me enough? Andreas, our entire dialogue was comprised of you usually warning me off something or the other. What we excelled in truly..." she raised her brows "...was nonverbal communication."

His chest rumbled with his quiet laughter while his fingers dipped into her hair. Prickling warmth spread down from that touch.

"I hate to diminish the impression you have of my power and influence," he added, and she snorted, which in turn made him grin, "but Drakonite law prevents me from divorcing you for at least eighteen months."

She didn't even panic anymore. "So I have eighteen months to bring you to heel then?" She traced the flat of his brow with the tip of her finger. "I'd better start taking inventory of the weapons I can use against you."

"You've become bolder, *pethi mou*." His fingers dug into her flesh, feral hunger blazing in his eyes. "I didn't think it possible."

Her skin prickled with answering need. How could she forget that the harsher his control, the deeper his need for her?

"You and I will celebrate a jubilee even as the only King and Queen of Drakon together in two hundred years because I intend to prove that Theos was wrong."

"You said he didn't control you anymore. And what do you mean jubilee?"

"For two hundred years, there hasn't been a jubilee celebration. And no, Theos does not control me," he said cryptically. She hated the harshness that came into his eyes every time they talked of his father. The patrician features tightened, the easy humor fell. "Giving you up, giving up on this marriage will mean he wins, *agapita*. And I could not let Theos win. I could not let him be right…"

"Revenge against your dead father is no more a better foundation for marriage than an inexplicable obsession is. It will never work."

"It will work because I refuse to give in.

"If you truly are dedicated to making a difference in the world, if you really care so much about the work you did at that legal aid agency, you could do it from here.

"You could have the prestige and power of the King's Palace behind you. Or lead the pampered life of a queen.

"Find your place in my world, Ariana. I do not care what it is. But stop running away from me and from yourself."

Ariana stared, tremors running through her.

Every time she thought she finally understood him, he went and did something like this. And yet, she was beginning to understand him, beginning to see how his mind worked.

Andreas didn't know how to handle guilt any more than he knew how to handle the little something he had felt for her back then. So this opening to her. Not because he thought it was important to her or because her happiness mattered to him.

Yet, here was the perfect way to know whether they could ever work, the chance to pit the Ariana she was now against the future King's personality. The chance to see if that connection that had brought them together years ago could mean anything.

The chance, as he said, to prove the great King Theos wrong when he had called her a curse upon his heir's life.

"You're on, Your Highness," she whispered.

Hands crawling up his chest, rising to her toes, she touched her mouth to his.

For a few seconds, he was stiff, shock tensing his entire body against her. But Ari didn't care. She needed a taste of him, she needed courage to see this thing between them through.

His mouth was hard and unyielding but this time, she knew. She knew what simmered beneath that stoic, unaffected exterior. She knew the raw passion that dwelled under the academic's soul.

Hands perched on his shoulders, she licked the seam of those sculpted lips. When he growled, when he roused out of that momentary freeze, she swiped her tongue inside his mouth. Nibbled at his lower lip.

Heat poured through her in liquid rivulets, pooling in her lower belly.

And just when his hands descended to her hips, just as he slammed her chest against his, Ari somehow managed to slip away from his hold.

Breaths harsh, dark pupils wide, he scowled at her. "Come back here, Ari." The tension that poured out of his lean frame was a balm to her soul.

Holding his gaze, she made a show of wiping her mouth with the back of her hand. As if it was that simple to erase the taste and feel of him from her being. "No."

"No?"

She smiled, feeling a freedom, a joy she hadn't known in years. "That was just a small test for myself, Your Highness."

A vein fluttered at his temple. "A test?"

She nodded, loving his frustration in that moment. "A test to see if I still had it in me to bring you to your knees."

"And?"

Andreas Drakos reduced to blank questions…was there a sweeter victory? "Are you ready to fall to your knees, Your Highness?"

He said nothing. And yet the gleam in his eyes told her all she needed to know.

She still had it in her and this time, she was going to use it to design the life she wanted.

CHAPTER SEVEN

ARIANA SPENT THE first two weeks as Andreas's wife being swept up in the storm that was the King's Palace and the Crown Prince's life.

True to Andreas's warning, there had been no time to center herself before the news had been leaked that the Crown Prince had married in secret.

Had, against every popular opinion and to the shock of the populace of Drakon, fallen irrevocably in love.

A strategic leak by his own PR team, she'd learned later. A way to massage the truth.

All of Andreas's overseas trips now had a perfect explanation. Having accidentally met Ariana, a young beautiful lawyer, General Theseus Sakis's daughter, in the States, he had fallen violently in love with her and, due to some obscure legal obligations, had to marry immediately.

It was as if Drakon and its people had been hungry for some explanation like this about their Prince. The tale of their stoic Prince falling in love and marrying in secret seemed to fill a much-needed hole in the country's perception of him. Overnight, Andreas turned into a romantic figure, vulnerable as any of them.

The moment the formal press statement from him had hit the news cycle, Ariana was lost.

Invitations to balls, charity galas and state dinners began pouring in. Dress fittings, appearances by Andreas's side, private dinners with powerful members of the cabinet and Crown Council, Ariana held her own through it all.

Even as she realized that she was mostly ornamental on Andreas's arm, even as most of the times, the men—powerful traditionalists—talked as if she couldn't understand a word of import, even as she realized that the Queen's role was mostly titular, Ariana behaved with the perfect decorum.

And the shift in the perception about him, the picture his PR team painted of the Crown Prince's marriage enabled Andreas to make his own headway in the political zone.

Tax reforms that had been introduced temporarily passed through the cabinet. A host of new members were appointed to the Crown Council—most of them direct appointees handpicked by Andreas and Nikandros—small business owners, professors from universities, had been met with resistance but finally passed.

That he was serious about the changes he had spouted gave Ariana much to think about. She saw the power that rested in Andreas's hands, the duty of serving his country that he thought was inviolable. Saw the magic of it in Nikandros's round-the-clock efforts to make Drakon's economy sustainable, the pride and tears in Eleni's eyes as Andreas, against Gabriel's threats to kidnap her away from Drakon if she accepted, appointed her the executive chairwoman for the House of Drakos charities that involved millions of dollars.

More than once, she'd caught surprise, humor, even curiosity in Andreas's eyes as she acted the perfect hostess, the adoring spouse to the serious Prince. Almost as if he didn't believe the meek image she'd presented to the world.

Thanks to Eleni, she'd chosen a stylist that understood her personal style. Petra ran her life as smoothly as she did Andreas's and for now, Ariana relented control. Her first few public appearances with Andreas would define her future as the Queen and she toed the line. She might be a lawyer but she didn't know the intricacies of a political system like Drakon's so she listened and learned.

No one could find fault with her, not even the staunchest royal critics. Thanks to Eleni's constant advice and unrelenting support—once she'd learned that Ariana meant to stay—she'd sailed through those first two weeks. Even King Theos would have been surprised.

Everything went great except one thing.

All the time she'd spent with Andreas could be counted down to minutes. Their exchanges limited to discussing the weather, which had turned dismally cold.

Nothing personal touched their words. At the end of the day, they retired to separate chambers, even as tension seeped through the very air between them.

Ariana saw his desperate need for her in his restrained touches, in the hot, hungry look he leveled her way even in the midst of a crowd. Felt the answering shudder of her own body.

He wanted her, and yet he'd barely said two words to her since that evening. Barely shared the pressures of his life, the constant stress that he must be under. What he wanted, again, was relief and she was damned if she was going to be it. Damned if she was going to let him slot her again.

It suited her just fine, she told herself. She didn't need him to hold her hand through her new life. She definitely didn't feel deserted when he left on a trip to Asia without so much as a goodbye.

It was her own naïveté in not realizing how busy his life was. In not understanding that Andreas could never truly belong to anyone. After the storm of the first couple of weeks, she finally had a moment to breathe. And her own plans to make, so she shut up that internal voice that said nothing had changed and threw herself into her work.

Only it wasn't that simple. Going up against Andreas and his will, she should've known, would never be simple. She wanted to learn more of Drakon, she needed to be more than an accessorized, haute-couture figurehead.

The first wake-up call came in the third week, when she'd decided to visit a woman's shelter in the capital city.

Petra had relayed the answer. *His Highness feels that such a visit would not be wise in the current time.*

Somehow, Ariana had kept her cool.

Then, she had decided to scout for premises near the palace where she could set up her legal offices. Before she could set a foot out of the palace, security had waylaid her.

His Highness has ordered an apartment to be

*cleared for Mrs. Drakos's use in the South Wing of
the palace.*

A mansion of a wing, attached to a team of lawyers who would do the grunt work while bearing the
stamp of her name.

Somehow, she had kept her temper.

Next, she'd been drafted, without her agreement, to
an afternoon tea with a host of powerful patronesses
of charities from Drakon. Ariana had managed to not
choke on the tea.

Next, the interview she'd given to a press member about her background in law dealing with do-
mestic disputes and her aspirations to start a legal aid
agency in Drakon had been sanitized until Ariana had
sounded like a mouthpiece for the palace and a color-
ful accessory that belonged on Andreas's arm.

The last straw came when she'd learned, through
a slip by Petra, that all the calls she'd been receiving
from her friend Rhonda, whose divorce case had been
pulled up on the calendar, had been rerouted without
a word to her.

Ariana had had enough.

It had taken him mere weeks to revert back to type.
To relegate her to a small part of his life. To turn her
into nothing but a figurehead. *Thee mou,* if all he'd
wanted was a placeholder, why had he gone to the
lengths of kidnapping her? Why make her those promises?

God, she was a fool to have ever believed him, a
fool to hope that they could make this work, even without love complicating matters.

But this time, she would not run away, she told herself walking the perimeter back into the royal wing. If

he wasn't going to come to her, she would go to him. She knew he'd returned from his trip almost a day ago. And she was done waiting.

She pushed her way through the small corridor off her lounge and barged into the other master suite that was connected to hers through it.

She snarled at a sleekly dressed bodyguard when he blocked her in front of the massive double doors. "His Highness does not let anyone enter his private suite." When she raised a brow, the guard shrugged. "Not even his brother or sister."

"Did the Crown Prince have a wife before?" Ariana demanded in a soft, utterly privileged voice that would have surprised even her father.

After what seemed an eternity, the guard nodded, threw open the massive doors and moved aside.

Ariana stepped inside, blinked and came to a still. A faint thread of sandalwood and something so intrinsically Andreas curled through her muscles.

From the wide French doors on the side to the huge high windows, everything was covered with light-blocking blinds. She rubbed her arms. The room was cool.

Dark mahogany wood, almost black furniture dotted around the vast semi-circular room. A wide desk sat next to the French doors, which would open to a view of the mountain range in the distance, she knew. Not a single pen or paper was out of place on the gleaming wood yet there were reams of paper-work on it.

In the center, the room retreated farther back. Darker and quieter than the rest. Did it lead to his bedroom?

Pulse zigzagging, Ariana forced herself to look away.

One whole wall behind her was floor-to-ceiling bookshelves. She didn't need to go close to see they would be books mostly on the history of Drakon, and the history of the world, neatly filed in alphabetical order.

Moving on feet that felt no reticence, she went to the bookshelf. Her fingers, she noted, were trembling as she ran them over the spines of some familiar titles. Warmth filled her limbs, the books greeting her like old friends.

They were, in a way. All the months he'd spent at the fishing village, these books had been in the library of the Drakos estate. She'd gotten so used to seeing him carry them around, she had one day asked him to talk about them.

A whole new side of the Crown Prince had been revealed to her when he spoke of history with passion, wonder, a love in his voice that she'd never thought him capable of.

She moved along the shelves, sometimes smiling at a familiar title, sometimes frowning. Until a title hit her like an invisible punch.

Dragon Captured: A New Look at the Ancient Lore of Drakon, by Andreas Titus Drakos.

Ariana plucked it from the shelf, heart thumping hard against her rib cage. The book he'd been writing when he'd taken the sabbatical.

Why had he lied?

The gilded spine, the crisply expensive paper told its own story. It was a customized collector's edition. It had been his dream to share his love for the history of his country with the world.

That rich, new-book scent stole into Ari's blood as she slowly flicked the thick jacket open. She traced the title and his name on the inside with shaking fingers. Turned another page and her heart jumped into her throat.

For the girl who loved me.

The book fell from Ari's hands and landed on the thick carpet with a muffled thump. She fell to her knees, tears making big splotches on the thick paper. A silent sob falling from her mouth, she picked up the picture that had fallen out of the book when it landed.

It was her. She didn't even remember when it was taken. Her body was turned away from the camera, her hands full with a tray of dark coffee and a slice of oozing baklava.

The same thing that Andreas had ordered every day for months in the café.

But her face was turned toward the camera, that big, goofy, wide grin curving her mouth. Her hip jutting out at a cocky angle, her entire body screamed a sultry invitation, and her eyes were warm and sparkling.

Thee mou, she'd been audacious, teasing and taunting the Crown Prince like that. She'd been bold and brave, grabbing what she wanted from life. Something she'd forgotten. She folded her legs under her and sat on the thick carpet, the picture in her hands, the book sprawled open in her lap.

She read a few pages here and there and smiled, hearing his passion in his words. She traced the lines of her own face in the picture, worn-out and fading, a startling contrast among the crisp, new pages of the book.

Had Andreas looked at that picture again and again? Her mind raced, aided by her heart, raring to jump to all sorts of conclusions.

Like a leaf in a storm, she sat there. Guilt and hope vied. There it was, the proof that maybe Andreas had cared. A little. At least after he'd thought she'd died, said a bitter voice, the voice that wanted to keep her safe.

No, this was proof that his heart had not been carved from the same rock on which his palace sat. Something that had hardened in her chest loosened. The guilt that she had carried along for so long…it thawed at the sight of that rumpled picture.

She replaced the picture in the book and the book on the shelf. On legs that felt like jelly, she ventured deeper into the suite.

The room was cavernous, with soaring ceilings that seemed like they could touch the sky. The huge skylight had dark shades.

The king-sized bed with a cream upholstered headboard and pristine white sheets beckoned to her. Andreas slept on his stomach on one side of the bed, the sheets up to his waist. Leanly muscled, his bare back was strikingly dark against the white sheets.

A smile broke through her at the sight of his large feet peeping out of the sheets. No couch or bed or sheets were ever tall enough for Andreas. Her sheets had looked like a child's blankets on him.

Ariana moved to the head of the bed, pulled by an urge she couldn't understand, much less fight. He had left her to fume and he was sleeping?

Then it came to her. He was used to not sleeping for days, went into that intense focus mode when an

important matter came up and then he would crash,
sleep through the day and night.

His face was to the side on the pillow, his arms
under it. Even in the dark, she could make out those
distinctive features. Impossibly long lashes fanned toward the slope of his cheekbones. His mouth, a rigid,
stiff line, was relaxed into a soft curve. She ran a finger over the impossibly sharp bridge of his nose, traced
the wing of his eyebrows, the defined line of his jaw.

Something fluid and desperate, a twisted longing
rose through her. For weeks now, she'd been racking
her mind as to why she'd run away like that, why she'd
had to take her guardian's help, whom she had never
liked, to flee Andreas.

Why hadn't she just stayed and made him understand what he'd been doing to her?

Now she knew. A part of her was always going to
be weak when it came to him. A part of her was always going to be that eighteen-year-old who'd fallen
in love with him. A part of her was always going to
hope that maybe, just maybe, he would love her a little.

She needed to walk out of here and think, she—

Long fingers wrapped around her wrist, arresting
her, half prostrate over him and the bed. She slapped
a hand over her mouth, but it was too late. Black eyes,
that shouldn't have been shining in the dark, stared
at her, sleep diluting the usual forbidding expression.

"Ari? What's wrong?" His voice was husky and
sleep-mussed. Like he had sounded after sex.

"Nothing…is wrong." The sheets slithered around
him as he blinked and moved to his side, his eyes still
adjusting to the darkness. "I…didn't mean to disturb
you. Go back to sleep."

Desperate to escape, Ariana wiggled in his grip, but it tightened. She gasped when his arms went under her shoulders and tugged her onto the bed.

His dark face hovered over hers, his sleek, taut body propped on his elbows, his breath hitting her nose in soft strokes. Not even out of breath as he watched her like that, his body a heated canopy over hers.

"It is hard enough to sleep knowing you are in the next suite, *finally*, after all these months. You should know better than to taunt me in my own bed."

Her hands rose to his shoulders to push him off. Hard and tense, he was like velvet-covered rock under her questing fingers. Heat swirled and pooled in her lower belly and she shook from head to toe. Standing on the edge of the abyss. Waiting to fall.

That faded picture of her, hidden away in a book he hadn't showed to the world, beckoned like a beacon.

Their eyes met and held in the dense dark, that connection, always so strong between them, tangible again. Oh, but with his legendary self-control in play, he did not kiss her. He would not break his promise. Would not give in until she asked. She could see the desire in his glowing eyes, in the flaring of his patrician nose.

"Ask me to kiss you." Clipped and serrated. On edge. Only the Crown Prince of Drakon could make a request sound like an arrogant command. His body was tense, his breath, because she knew him so well, a little shy of normal. "*Diavole*. Ask me to kiss you, Ari."

CHAPTER EIGHT

ARIANA LICKED HER LIPS, longing cleaving her in half.

This, him. This fire that he invoked with a single look. It was all she'd been missing in her life.

"Kiss me," she said simply, throwing herself off the cliff.

His arms on either side of her head, his fingers digging into her hair tight, he slanted his mouth over hers. Tiny, numerous frissons shook through her body at that first contact. Firm and supremely male, his lips touched her in a soft, silken, barely there caress that was nowhere near enough.

A taste of whiskey and him. Fingers tracing his collarbone, Ariana shook all over.

Another butterfly-soft brush, there and gone again.

A sweep of his tongue over the seam, and then nothing.

Slow kisses. Soft kisses. Testing the suppleness of her lips. Tempting to steal her breath. Again and again. Over and over.

Her body bucked off the bed, seeking more, needing more. "*Please*, Andreas," she whispered half sobbing, every nerve ending taut with hunger.

A taunting smile breaking out on his mouth, Andreas moved to his side, and threw a muscled leg over hers. Rock-hard thigh pressed hers into the bed, a languorous weight that her body craved. "I've forgotten how much it pleases me when you say please."

"I have forgotten how much I hated you in bed."

"I have had two years to imagine this, Ariana. You've had days." Pure devil glinted in his wide smile. "Now that you're here, I intend to take my time."

His arms sidled under her as if she were a featherweight, tugging her onto her side. A long finger traced a lazy trail along the neckline of her loose T-shirt. Her breasts were thrust up, the upper curves visible through the hanging neckline. Up and down, until the pulse at her neck throbbed violently.

Anticipation was fire in every muscle every time his finger skated the edge of one curve. *Thee mou*, he'd adored her breasts. Worshipped them. So much so that she had once orgasmed just with his mouth on them.

The memory slid over skin like a silky caress. Fired nerve endings.

His finger hovered over the upper curve of one breast, his breath a harsh whisper. "Your body has changed."

A profound ache twisted through her. All she could do was nod.. Even as fear whispered over her spine, she needed this intimacy. Craved it for so long. Here, in the dark, the world shut away, maybe she'd find the man she'd fallen in love with.

Jet-black eyes held hers, possessive and powerful. "It turns me on even more." She saw the edge of that hunger in his eyes, the deep grooves of need around his mouth. "Although, nothing could turn me on faster than seeing how eager you always were."

She lifted her hands to his face. With the pad of her thumb, she traced the long curve of his lower lip. A stern, stiff line until he smiled. Or kissed. "And you were never desperate enough."

He frowned, but Ariana had had enough of the power play. She needed to know if it was as magical as it had been back then. She needed to know if this heat between them was worth burning herself all over again.

Sending her seeking fingers into his hair, she tugged his arrogant head down. Breath rushing in and out, she licked that sensual lower lip with the tip of her tongue. His growl reverberated from his hard chest. Without waiting, she opened her mouth over his and dragged it from one end to the other. Another growl, a warning. She didn't heed it. She kissed him again and again, until heat sparked where their lips touched, until she was out of breath. Until her lips stung.

Until the need to shatter that control was a scream in her blood. She dragged that lower lip between her teeth and then flicked her tongue over it. The curse he spewed was a balm over her heated skin. In a fraction of a second, she was pushed onto her back and his mouth crushed hers.

Her upper lip banged against her teeth. Her scalp prickled at how tightly he gripped her with one hand, while the other clasped her jaw, holding her still for his assault.

Spotlights filled her vision as the taste of him exploded through her body. There were no more games, no more teasing. Angling his head, he deepened the pressure until the heat of their fused mouths was enough to scald them both.

With a stark groan, she opened her mouth. He swooped in. The slide of his tongue as it chased hers was so erotic that her toes dug into the sheets. Again and again, he devoured her mouth, his wicked tongue dipping in and out with a frenetic rhythm that her body recognized. Craved.

His hands gripped her hair tight, his mouth opening and closing over hers, sucking and nipping, until she was trembling with a fever beneath him.

Until the taste of him was forever embedded in her.

She had no control over herself, no will of her own. She was begging with her body, her hips thrusting into empty air. His hands moved down to her shoulders, between her heavy breasts and then down to her abdomen. Again and again, up and down, touching, marking, staking a claim, while he ravished her mouth. Stroking her body higher and higher, promising her that cataclysm, enslaving her will.

"Tell me you need more, little wife." His tongue traced the rim of her ear in a silken stroke that had her clutching her thighs tight. The tip of it moved behind her ear, before his teeth caught her lobe. "Tell me where you want my hands and my mouth." A wicked, wild promise in a deep, husky voice she barely recognized as his.

His hand lay palm down on her chest, the tips of his long fingers touching her neck. Her heart thundered against this palm. Her breasts swelled, begging to be cupped in those powerful hands. Her nipples ached to be sucked into that mouth.

And he missed nothing.

His gaze flicked down toward the tight tips of her breasts visible through the thin fabric of her top, the trembling of her body, the tight clutch of her thighs. Naked satisfaction lined the angles of his gorgeous face. "Ask me to be inside you, Ari. *Dio*, my mouth, my hands, whatever you want, wherever you want."

Her entire body was screaming her need for him, her desire evident in her shallow breaths. And yet, for the devil in him, it was not enough.

He moved his hand down her stomach, down her pelvis until it rested over her mound. Her hips jerked against his fingers resting against the covered lips of her sex. Wetness drenched her panties, a fact he knew. For a dark strip of color scoured his sharp cheekbones.

"Ask me, Ariana." His voice fell to a whisper. His lashes fell and rose slowly. His breath a soft hiss in the dark. "I will do it with pleasure."

How was it that he gave her the power and yet it was Ari that was falling?

His body next to her was a fortress of need, yet controlled with that ironclad will. Ariana pushed her hip into him. He jerked back, his fingers digging into her hips. Arresting her movements. But too late.

She had felt the evidence of his desire. Her breath slowed, the faint tremor in his powerful shoulders telling her how on edge he was.

Only his control was better. Over his body, over his mind, always. He would never let himself lose that will.

She hadn't seen that back then. She hadn't realized that it pervaded every part of his life. Hadn't understood that for the Crown Prince of Drakon losing control of himself in bed was akin to giving Ariana a real place in his life. That it would mean him needing Ariana and not just the other way around.

The more she'd asked him for his attention, his time, the more he'd distanced himself. As if he didn't know what to do with her. As if she didn't fit in the neat box he'd made for her.

Needing her meant giving her power over himself, over his emotions.

And he was doing it again. He was compartmentalizing her because she made him feel.

Why had King Theos been so worried about him? Andreas's heart was stone.

A laugh erupted from her mouth. Whereas she... Ten years hadn't made a dent on the wants of her foolish heart. Every inch of her body, every beat of her heart wanted to grab this chance with him again. Wanted to find that happiness, that sense of completeness she had had with him in that village.

But not on his terms. Not at the cost of losing herself.

"*Oxhi,* Andreas," she managed, her lips stinging from the heat of his lips. The sound of her denial, somehow given voice, filled up her lagging will.

His hand didn't move from her sex. For a few seconds, Ari wondered if he'd even heard her. He looked up. A flash of consternation in his eyes before he exhaled roughly and buried his face in the valley between her breasts.

The damp warmth of his mouth made her nipples poke through her T-shirt. Ariana shivered, unraveling over the strength it took to resist him.

"I said no, Andreas." Steady and almost assertive. "Possible you don't understand the word because you've never heard it. Especially from me."

His laughter, muffled against her body, sent tremors

through her. Eyes glinting with humor, he stared at her. But the curiosity was there. He was taken aback by her refusal, she was sure. "You and I both know why you walked into my suite, Ariana." A sultry dare. "I have never held your desire for me against you."

So sure of her always. So sure of her devotion, of her hunger for him. Once he'd given in to their desire, she hadn't challenged him in any way. Wherever he had led with that arrogant confidence, she had blindly followed. When he'd decided they would marry, decided not asked, she'd happily forgotten all her dreams.

Because, of course, this worldly, powerful, sophisticated Crown Prince of Drakon, a man women lost their hearts to, had chosen her.

Her.

No wonder he'd thought she was another part in his privileged life. She jerked away from under him, his supreme arrogance lighting a fire in her. "You're an arrogant bastard, did I ever tell you that, Your Highness?"

"No." He pushed his hand through his hair roughly. Harsh and accented. She could have laughed at the irate expression on his face if her mind wasn't jumping from thought to thought. "You're right. For a minute there, I forgot that you hate me now.

"You'd never have ventured into my room without a reason. Not unless you were desperate."

"You're doing it again." She cringed at the anger in her voice.

"I don't understand."

"You ripped me from my life, brought me to this palace, and you go on your merry way. *Again.*" For the life of her, she couldn't stop the last word from tumbling out.

His stillness betrayed his shock. "Ari, help me understand."

He'd never used that tone with her. He had ordered her around, he'd dared her. He'd condescended to her. But never had he asked her in that tender voice. As if it really mattered to him.

"Ari, so help me God, if you don't explain yourself, I will—"

"What? You will lock me up?" she said on a laugh. "I can at least count on you to buck me back up." She sighed. "If all you wanted was a placeholder, why go to the trouble of kidnapping me? Why make promises to me?"

He truly looked so disconcerted that Ariana didn't know whether to laugh or cry. He pushed up on the bed. The sheet slithered to his waist, baring his torso. Lean, ropey muscle stretched tight over his abdomen when he sighed. "If this is about me not breaking down the door to your suite and ravishing you in your bed—"

"I'm not talking about sex. Is that all the use you see for me?"

"By your own admission, I needn't declare you Queen in front of the whole world if all I wanted was to screw you." The words were like tremors on the ground. So softly spoken but powerful enough to pull the ground from under her. He pushed a hand through his hair roughly.

Already trying to patch the little rip in his self-control. Already putting the veneer of civility over the confusion she saw in his eyes. The strain his desire for her put in his face.

Ari slowly got off the bed, every inch of her balking at walking away from sure pleasure. But she wouldn't be able to deny him or herself another time. And sleeping with Andreas when he saw no other use for her was like signing away her soul. Again.

And she couldn't do that.

Every cell in her wanted to grab this chance fate had given them both.

No, not fate. Andreas had done this. She didn't care that he called it payback for what she'd done to him.

He'd come for her. From what Nikandros had said, Andreas had scoured the world for her for two years, while Theos had clammed up. At the cost of risking his duties to the crown.

Of course, the man didn't know what it was to love. But to the best of his ability, Andreas had kept that commitment he had made to her. Was it his fault she wanted what he couldn't give?

"You promised me I could carve whatever role I want in your life, in this life, and yet you...you deny me every step of the way.

"I don't think you quite know what to do with me."

"What the hell does that mean?"

"You denied my visit to the women's shelter."

"It is not safe for you." His jaw tightened. "And damn it, Ari, you made the trip anyway. You drove the security staff nuts with your little stunt."

She tilted her chin up, raring to go at him. "You forced me to it. Just as you created office space for me in the palace. In a bloody wing of the palace, Andreas. My career is not a joke."

"As my wife and Queen, you will be far too busy to take up a full practice. This way—"

She pushed her face into his, her blood running hot now. "Did I let you down in any way? Did I not act as the perfect ornamental wife?"

His mouth twitched. Finally, he was catching on. "I couldn't believe my own eyes that it was you. So biddable and meek." He took a step forward. The predatory glint in his eyes sent sparks up her spine and she took a step backward. "All I could think of was whether I wanted you like that in bed."

"Andreas, I… I will do everything you need as your wife. But it doesn't mean I'll give up a single part of my life. It doesn't mean I'll let you or your staff decide how I live my life. I…can't…*we can't* make the same mistakes all over again."

"Kala," he said, almost conciliatory in his tone. "Tell me what you want from me to achieve that."

She straightened her spine. "For starters, I want my laptop, my personal belongings and my case files. I need to speak to Magnus. I want someone allotted to me, someone other than Petra, to see to my needs."

Every spark of humor disappeared. "No."

"What do you think I'll do over Skype, Andreas? Disappear like they do on spaceships? Have Skype sex with the man I lied to for ten years?"

"I do not like another man's name and the word *sex* together on your mouth, *agapi mou*. If you want to negotiate with me, you should know better than to provoke my ire."

"There are things I can do to help Magnus, until he finds a replacement. A couple of the cases, those two women are my friends. The law does very little to protect them from their powerful, abusive husbands.

Too many people have already let them down. I refuse to be one.

"I can't just disappear off the face of earth and let them believe the worst.

"You have your commitments and I have mine."

The lines around his mouth deepened. His dark eyes became flat, all that emotion wiped away. But Ariana was beginning to learn his cues again. The harder something hit him, the more shuttered he became. As if he could only implode. As if showing that emotion meant actually feeling it.

As if it were handing a weapon to Theos to use against him.

He pressed his fingers to his temple, his jaw clenched so tight that it might break. "Is that what I did to you, what motivated you to study law? Were you afraid of me, Ari?"

"What? No, of course not." The truth that she had left unsaid glimmered like a phantom around the room, sending a cold whisper through her. When his expression didn't budge, she hurried on. "For years, I was directionless. I hated my father for forcing things on me, so I never even discovered what I would enjoy, what I would be good at. I joined Magnus's legal aid agency as a clerk. Literally my job was to keep the filing in order.

"The more I saw the women that came through the agency's doors, the more I thought of my mother. My father never beat her, as some of those women were, but he…abused her just the same and I was powerless then.

"But I realized I could change that. I worked hard to get my law degree.

"I can still provide help to Magnus with the paperwork. And I want a couple of my friends to be flown here. Rhonda is going through a rough patch and Julia has no place to stay since her husband froze all their assets until the divorce proceedings finish."

Something like shock filled his eyes and Ariana felt a surge of satisfaction. Clearly, until this moment, he hadn't taken her seriously. "Here where?"

"To Drakon. To the King's Palace."

"You want me to provide sanctuary for two women who are running away from their husbands, and maybe even the law? To turn the palace into…some sort of pseudo-shelter?"

"I want to invite a couple of my good friends so that they can reassure themselves that the husband I have been hiding from for ten years is not a complete monster. And yes, they get a vacation.

"There have to be some perks to being the Crown Prince's precious wife, *ne*?"

"Kala," he said after a long gap. In a sudden movement that sent her heart lurching to her throat, he caged her against the wall. He took her mouth in a furious kiss that was all tongue and teeth and left her clinging to him. A sob burst out of her when he buried his mouth in her neck.

"Any more demands?"

Oh, his mouth was such a sensuous trap. So harsh when he dealt out commands and yet so soft when he kissed. She licked her lips and he leaned in closer, until his breath was a whisper across her heated skin. "I want Giannis back."

"Oxhi. Next?"

She placed her hands on his chest and pushed, determined to win this battle. "I want *my* people around me. People who care about *me*, people who don't think I'm your downfall. People who will stop me from feeling as if I live in a vacuum.

"I'm not a toy you play with, dress up and then put back on the shelf. That was me stopping before I fell into old, harmful patterns. I came—"

"Harmful patterns?" A vein pulsed dangerously at his temple. "Toy I played with? After every lie you've told, after everything you've done, I am still prepared to give you a place as my wife. A position coveted and sought out by the most beautiful, most accomplished women in the world today."

She flinched but refused to back down. "But you chose me. Whatever it is that sits in the place of your heart, wanted me, Andreas. In my own naive way, I didn't appreciate the magnitude of how uncharacteristic your choice was. How far off the mark you had gone."

She pushed against his hold on her wrists until her upper body grazed his. The hiss of his breath drowned her own. Jaw set, fingers taut over her wrists, he searched her face. As if he was seeing her for the first time.

"You still want me. You wish you didn't. And not just for a quick screw, or you would have taken me on the flight and dumped me. You could never be that ruthless with me then, and you won't now.

"Andreas Drakos has a weakness and it is me."

He pressed into her, a feral curve to his mouth. Bare chest crushed her breasts, and Ari threw her head back. Mouth drifting over her neck to the pulse, he smiled against her skin. "Point to Ariana Drakos. So why the hell are you not letting me give us both what we desperately need?"

"Because I'm not that train wreck reeling from her parents' deaths anymore. My primary function in life is not to provide you with sex and relief from your duties. I'm not awed that you noticed me, much less chose me." If her breath caught at the lies she was spouting, she hoped he didn't notice.

She twisted her hands in his grip and he let go, as if she'd burned him. But Ariana was not through. A fire ran in her veins, a sense of rightness that she belonged with him. A new hope that she could live with Andreas without losing herself.

She clasped his face in her hands, determined to make him see her.

"I'm not that girl who thought the sun and moon rose out of your eyes, Andreas. I will not be another cog in the machine of your life like Petra or Thomas or your chauffeur.

"Unless you're prepared to meet me as an equal, unless you're prepared to share your life with me, I'll run away again.

"And believe me, if I know one thing, it is how to escape from situations. This time, when you catch me—" his eyes gleamed at her acknowledgment "—I will come with a scandal that will rock your precious House of Drakos.

"So decide, Your Highness, if you want me in your life or not."

CHAPTER NINE

ANDREAS FORCED HIMSELF to let Ariana go, stripped off his drawstring pants and walked into the cold shower. The mosaic tiles were startlingly cold against his over-heated skin. He turned the jets to biting cold and still it took a few minutes for his arousal to abate, for his rational mind to grasp hold of the situation.

By the time he was out of the shower, he was shivering. He wrapped a towel around his waist and stood in front of the mirror.

His hair was overlong, falling past his ears. His eyes still had those dark shadows but had lost that bruised look he'd been walking around with for God knew how long. Gone too was that black void he'd carried inside of him for months.

And the black, biting, cold rage after Theos, in one of his mad rages, had spilled that Ariana was alive. It was as if his world was beginning to tilt back to normal again. He was beginning to understand that he had known nothing about her back then. Nothing of substance at least.

Even now, he knew there were things he still could not grasp. Things he knew he saw in her eyes when she had lain in bed next to him.

Things he struggled to put into words.

If you want me in your life, Your Highness…

Laughter, shocking even him, burst out of him at the audacity of the woman.

She had always been reckless and defiant, and yet there was something new to her. A self-possession that was as intoxicating as it forced him to pay attention.

She clearly thought he'd miss that adoration, and a part of him did. But this woman, who challenged him even as she trembled with her desire for him, she couldn't hold a candle to that girl.

He had no doubt she meant every word of her threat. No doubt that she would bring scandal, if not ruin, to his feet if he didn't give her whatever it was she wanted.

The challenge, instead of riling him, made anticipation flow in his veins.

He wanted to argue and negotiate with her. He wanted to dominate that defiance until it turned into desire. He wanted her under him, writhing and screaming.

Once he dressed, he could not however give her chase, as desperately as he wanted to.

The moment he had stepped out of his suite, Petra and his three aides had been desperate for his time. A contract he was signing with the House of Tharius came up and his thoughts veered.

His life would be so much better if he divorced her and took Maria Tharius for his wife. A doyenne of charities, Maria had been groomed since birth for a role like that. She would be amenable to his every wish, would know her place, be a proper mother for any children they had.

Maria would be the perfect Queen of Drakon. Maria would not demand that he give sanctuary to women fleeing their lives. Maria would not demand that he locate a security guard who worked in the palace ten years ago, who clearly had broken protocol and befriended the Crown Prince's young wife. Much less order that he not only be reinstated but join her personal team, knowing that it made her husband… uncomfortable that his wife was…chummy with that man.

Face it, Andreas. You're insanely jealous.

A growl rose through his throat and his team froze around him.

Dio, was this what she reduced him to?

In his heart of hearts, he knew Ariana wouldn't have cheated on him. And yet he'd been insanely jealous of her friendship with that young guard.

And he still was, given that Ariana clearly still had affection for Giannis.

He, the future King, jealous of a small-time guard.

Yet the thought of sitting down to dinner with Maria for the next thirty years, the thought of seeing Maria's placid smile across a crowded ballroom, a woman who would always remain a stranger because he just knew she'd stick to her place, the thought of taking her to bed… Distaste filled his mouth.

Thee mou, now that he had found her again, only Ariana would do.

Ariana, who had already won over his family with her effervescent personality.

Ariana, who would not give a damn about protocol and etiquette when it came to their own children. No, she would be the first one to slide down the side of a snow-covered hill. The one who would encourage them to break as many rules as possible. The one who would…love them unconditionally, whether they were an academic like him or a sick child like Nik had been. Or a little girl craving acceptance, like Eleni had been.

The one who would give a new definition to the future reputation of the House of Drakos.

"I want a Giannis Petrakis located as soon as possible," he said to one of his aides. "He used to be a security guard with the palace. Have him report to Mrs. Drakos."

"Mrs. Drakos?"

His aide paled when Andreas pinned him with a look. "Yes, Mrs. Drakos, my wife."

In the following week, he chose to avoid her, chose to immerse himself in the most pressing state matters. Tried to lose himself in the riot almost brewing among the members of the Crown Council after he had passed the latest edict, relinquishing them of their powerful positions.

His opening their real estate to Gabriel's company, and Nikandros's risky financial ventures, had already caused waves.

The people didn't understand investment when their national debt was already in millions of dollars. But Andreas had persisted.

It had taken everything he'd had to trust Nikandros, but he had. And it was the best decision he had made, for Gabriel's company had already boosted the employment rates in the remote areas of Drakon.

There were a hundred matters for him to see to.

Yet all he felt was this raw, fierce need to possess

her. To shatter the defiance he saw in her eyes, to own the fiercely strong woman she'd become.

To fix whatever she thought they had to fix between them so that he could drag her to bed and drive himself inside her.

She would be unlike any Queen Drakon had seen, yes. But at least she would not let him descend into that kind of megalomania that Theos had fallen into over the last few years. She would not let Andreas complete the transformation into becoming that hard man who, despite having all the riches and power in his hands, would forever remain alone in the end.

The man his father had forced him to become.

A man who would always be feared but never liked. Never loved.

He'd give her everything she asked for, this time. Everything that was in his power to give.

It was late evening almost a week later when Andreas was finally free. He'd had Petra invite Ariana to dine with him in his private suite. He was determined to be civil tonight, and not slide down the slippery path to their disturbing past.

They needed a fresh start and for that, he needed to believe Ariana. He needed to understand, as much as it burned him, that Ariana had left him because he'd made living with him unbearable.

He had barely time to shower after his long day and put on fresh clothes when Ariana walked into his suite.

A panorama of expressions crossed her face as her gaze fell on the intimate table set out on the veranda, overlooking the courtyard, with a spectacular view of the horizon. He tried to see it from her point of view. Crystalware twinkled in the orange glow of the setting sun. A bottle of champagne sat in an ice bucket. Their food was already sitting on the table since he'd dismissed the staff already.

"*Kalispera*, Ariana."

He saw her head come up but she didn't turn.

So easily she snagged at his temper. Until he saw the tense line of her shoulders. Until he remembered that this was Ariana and emotional control didn't come to her easily.

In fact, it was the opposite of her nature. Which had been what had attracted him to her in the first place.

His amazement that anyone could live with such free rein given to their emotions.

Knowing what he did now about her background, it amazed him even more how fearlessly she had lived then. How generously she had given of herself to anyone who had come into the sphere of her life.

She slowly turned toward him, as if she needed the extra minute to compose herself. Something caught in his chest, a twinge of regret maybe, for how things had been once. The wariness in her eyes...he was determined to push through it.

He wanted the old Ariana back. The Ariana who had worshipped him. The Ariana who would have never filtered anything that had come to her mouth, especially with him.

The Ariana that had made him feel that he was, finally, not alone. That he need not be alone.

"*Kalispera*, Andreas," she replied back softly. The wariness didn't abate but neither could she stop her gaze from devouring his face nor from sweeping down his body and back up. As if she had been starving for the sight of him.

Just as he'd been for her.

He felt no such compunction about showing his own interest, however. He had had a week from hell and all that had kept him going was that he would come back to this.

To her.

That tension that had become second skin flickered over his muscles as he swept his gaze over her.

She was dressed differently today, like the Ariana he remembered.

Sexy, confident, yet with a thread of vulnerability beneath.

A simple beige sheath dress that barely touched her knees, that made her golden skin glow with a burnished sheen. It showed off her toned arms and lithe figure with its simplicity. Black pumps made the most of her long, long legs, bringing her face almost to his chin.

Thee mou, he'd always loved how well she had fit against him. But now, that angular look was replaced by soft curves. Curves he wanted to feel beneath his body, softness he wanted to surround himself in.

She left her hair to fall softly around her shoulders. It softened that stubborn jaw of hers.

When their gazes met, he smiled and raised a brow. "You look gorgeous."

She flushed but held his gaze. "*Efharisto.* You look—" her mouth twitched, and so did his entire body in response "—very…dashing."

"Can I assume that the cold war between you and Petra reached its conclusion?"

"Let's just say we reached a mutually satisfactory agreement."

"What is that?"

"To stay out of each other's way. And now that I have my own people, her attitude doesn't bother me at all."

He frowned, remembering all the small tidbits she'd thrown out during the dinner with his family. The near panic he'd seen in her eyes as she'd stood by his bed.

"I have appointed Giannis as my aide and I've been interviewing candidates for an administrative assistant and a PR person. Eleni's miffed, I think, that I chose someone Mia recommended."

He half nodded, his mind still on the previous issue.

Knowing Petra's loyalty, and even her bit of possessiveness when it came to him, he didn't doubt the veracity of Ari's words. Regret, piling up as high as his guilt, made his voice harsh. "Petra is invaluable to me, *ne*. But not indispensable, Ariana.

"I will have her moved to another department instantly."

"Oxhi," she replied instantly but with such shock in her eyes that Andreas momentarily stilled. "Not necessary."

Christos, did she really think he would put a staff member before her, even now? After everything she'd told him about how isolated she'd felt then? About how Petra and her team had taken their lead from Theos's treatment of her, even from Andreas's own retreat as he'd struggled with his own emotions?

He reached her, refusing to let her shy away from him. "Why not?"

"Because it would mean that I'm still that insecure girl. It sends a message that I'm helpless and I hide behind your power." She lifted her chin. "I mean to hold my own, against you and against everyone in your world this time, Andreas."

He nodded, pride filling his very veins. She had come a long way from that girl and he needed to see that. "I think you've already proved that."

"I could not believe it when Petra told me you wanted to dine with me. Now I'm astonished that you went to this much trouble."

"Why?"

"For one thing, I know how busy you are. And for another, I didn't think you would take my ultimatum seriously. But I guess that's the one chink in your armor, *ne*? That I might somehow go to the media. In the current sentiment the people have with you, a woman crying kidnapping is the last thing you need."

He poured them both a glass of the champagne and handed it to her. "So let me get this straight." A thread of chill filled his tone and her head jerked up. "The only reason I'd want to spend time with you is for damage control."

Her white knuckles around the champagne flute were the only sign that she wasn't as breezy as she sounded. "Is it not?"

"No, Ariana." He put his glass on the table with not quite a steady hand, and then took hers. Then he went and stood in front of her. He plucked the small velvet box he'd had his aide retrieve from the royal treasury and held it out.

She didn't look up but her chest fell and rose with her shallow breaths. He waited, knowing in that moment how much he had crushed her tender heart ten years ago.

How he'd done exactly what he'd feared he would do.

"Ari, look at me." When she didn't, his patience finally unraveled its last thread. Clasping her chin with both his hands, he tilted it up.

Whatever he meant to say fluttered away at the sight of her lush lips. Angling his head, he took her mouth with a hunger that punched through him.

Thee mou, he'd forgotten how sweet, how perfect she tasted. Lust surged through him as she swept her tongue over his lower lip.

No reluctance, no hesitation.

No lies, no dares.

Pure Ariana, pouring every inch of her emotion into the kiss, right down to the hoarse chuckle when their teeth banged in their hurry to get at each other.

But Andreas was not in a laughing mood today.

He was in a devouring mood. *Dios*, he'd waited so long for the taste of her. So long to feel like he would combust if he didn't slide inside her wet warmth.

Her hands moved to his chest, her body arching like a bow toward him.

The more he took of her mouth, the more he needed. Wrapping his hand around her neck, holding her still, he licked and stroked with his tongue, bit and suckled with his teeth, until she was whimpering against him. Trembling with need.

The kiss flared higher and hotter. The dinner was forgotten. Promises he'd made misting in the heat of their passion.

The press of her breasts against his chest, her long thighs straddled by his own, that scent of her skin…it was like striking a match to hot cinders.

He moved his hands to her hips and then to the

curve of her buttocks. Roughly, he pulled her until she was plastered to his lower body.

His erection lengthened.

She moaned and arched into his touch, always so responsive. Always pushing Andreas toward a bit more madness.

He lifted her on the next breath and arranged her on the table. The ice bucket clattered to the ground with an almighty thud, the slide of ice cubes on the concrete a hiss in the silence.

She was breathing hard, her eyes heavy lidded, a protest on her lips, he knew. She meant to talk, throw up another one of her demands. Or dares.

He didn't let her get the words out. Instead, he stole them from her lips in another kiss that had them both growling against each other.

Thee mou, he wanted her like this—spread out on the table on a veranda of the King's Palace where sky and the stars would know that she was his. Her dress had already bunched up her thighs, giving him easy access to soft, silky skin. One hand sliding up her thighs, he buried the other in her hair and tugged her up.

Eyes glossed over, mouth trembling, she was utterly beautiful.

"I'm going to touch you, *glykia mou*," he whispered at her ear. "I'm going to see if you're wet for me already or not."

He held her against his chest while his fingers found the dampness through the thin fabric of her panties. Fire spewed in his muscles, his erection pressing persistently against his trousers. *Christos*, she was so ready, so wet for him. Burying his mouth in her temple, he pushed a finger into her sex and she jerked against him.

"Andreas, *parakalo*…" Head thrown back, she pushed her hips against his hand when he pressed his thumb against her swollen clit. A sob fell from her lips. The setting sun made her flushed skin shimmer like pure gold. His fingers had made a mess of her hair. Beads of sweat dotted above her lip. He licked that lush lip. The scent of her arousal spread through his blood like a drug.

He tugged the neckline of the forgiving sheath and growled at the sight of her bare breast. He gave the brown puckered tip a lick and her spine arched hungrily.

Her fingers moved to his hair and he complied. He rubbed his jaw against the wet tip before he closed his mouth and sucked.

She was close now. He could feel her body swelling around his fingers. The muscles in her pelvis tightening against the very pleasure she craved.

"You did not wear a bra," he whispered against her skin before he laved the plump nipple again. "Tell me, Ariana, that it was for me. Tell me that was because you knew how mindless I go at the sight of your breasts."

Her eyes flew open, unfocused, sluggish, before they settled on him. Desire made them glitter like the finest gems. An impish smile curved her mouth. "The material…it shows straps. Not for you."

Even now, she denied him that satisfaction.

He hooked his finger inside her tight entrance and waited, breath punching through him like bellows. She shuddered against him, and let out a slew of curses that had laughter thunder through him.

Her hands clutched his wrists, and her lithe body

pushed against him. "Yes, okay. I went without a bra for you, *kala*. *Parakalo*, Andreas. More."

Fierce satisfaction raging through him, he pumped his fingers into that fast rhythm her body loved. He intended to dismantle all the defenses she had built. He intended to have that Ari of old again.

Her body tensed and bucked, like a boat flung against the waves. Sounds ripped from her throat, needy and raw. Bending his mouth, he nuzzled at her breast and like Independence Day fireworks, she fell apart around him with a keening moan.

Her thighs trapped his hand between them, her breath still harsh for several seconds.

She fell into his chest like someone had removed the bones from her body. Andreas pulled the dress up to cover her breasts, his own body screaming for release. And yet, utterly satisfied on another level. He swept his gaze over her, that possessive instinct she always brought out in him in full riot.

Long, quivering limbs, golden skin flushed, a smile hovering about her lips, her sensual repose was just as arousing as her uninhibited response.

On a deep level he didn't even try to understand, he felt as if his world was finally being righted.

From the moment he'd seen her standing in front of the city hall, her face pale, a stricken look in her eyes, he'd needed this.

He had needed to see her splinter with pleasure, pleasure he gave.

He had needed to know that Ariana was still his.

She opened her mouth and pressed a kiss to his chest, creating a damp patch. "I..." Her sigh whispered over his skin, his shirt no barrier to sensations. Another openmouthed kiss against his abdomen. Which clenched like a steel wall. Her hands moved over him, stroking, touching, questing with a possessive flair that was more revelatory of Ariana than anything else. "What was that about?"

He tilted her chin up. "If you're asking me questions, clearly it was not that good."

Ripples of her laughter shook her slender frame. "Oh, believe me, it was an earthquake. But I still want to know...what—"

"That was about the present."

She looked up, and frowned. "What?"

He couldn't help himself. He dipped his head and kissed her swollen lips again. "Neither the past, nor the future. It was about now." He tucked a defiant curl behind her ear and stared into her eyes. The words came so easily to his lips. So clearly. "I wanted to kiss you, Ari. I wanted to see you shatter in my arms and I followed that urge."

The most beautiful smile spread over her face, something almost incandescent flickering in her eyes. That quality that defined Ariana. That quality that he wanted pervading his own life.

She nodded, clasped his jaw and kissed him softly. Slowly. As if she never wanted the moment to end.

A feeling he was coming to recognize within himself.

"Going with that urge was good. Andreas Drakos giving in to urges is *very* good. Provoking you to that urge—man, I feel on top of the world." She ran a finger over his lips, tracing them over and over. "I... have an urge, too." He held his breath as her hands traveled down his chest, past his trousers and slowly came to rest on his groin. He became still, arousal spiking through him as she traced his shape. "We can't go to bed yet, but your wife has other means to satisfy you."

How he managed to hold her fingers from wreaking havoc on him, he had no idea. Even he was impressed by his willpower. His erection throbbed in rhythm with his heart, his breath serrated. "Why can't we go to bed, exactly?" he asked softly. He hadn't planned any of this. He hadn't even meant to touch her until things between them had reached a new stage. But, of course, in his relationship with Ariana, passion had been one of the things that had always been right.

But now that she denied him, he wanted to know why.

A shadow passed across her face, though she tried to cover it up. "I started my pills again just the other day. So we won't be protected."

"Protected against what? I'm clean."

"Against pregnancy," she answered in a soft voice.

The moment stretched through awkwardness and fell directly into something altogether painful.

When he waited with a raised brow, she moved back from him. An edge to her movements, she straightened her dress, careful not to meet his gaze.

A shiver snaked up his spine. "There is something called a condom."

She shrugged and ran a hand through her hair. Straightened her already perfect dress a little more. Buying time. "You hate condoms. More importantly, condoms are not foolproof. Nothing, actually, is foolproof."

Déjà vu hit him like a strike to his solar plexus.

"Ariana…" he said but arrested anything that wanted to come out.

He ran a hand over his face, tension corkscrewing through him.

They had been through this once before. Their biggest, dirtiest fight when he'd asked her to get off the birth control pills.

The closest he'd ever come to losing his self-control because of course, she had absolutely refused to do so. And then his threat that he would not sleep with her unless she did.

Dios, he had been like a wounded beast.

Of course, Ariana could never take a dare lying down. They had ended up in a heap in front of the fireplace, clinging to each other after the stormy sex and having realized that something had been broken irrevocably between them.

The only time, the single time, sex had been something other than a source of joy between them.

He had left for the oil summit three days after that without a word to her. And when he'd returned, she'd disappeared from his life.

He had used sex against her, corrupted the only pure thing between them.

Desperation, he realized now, had clouded reason, good judgment. And *Thee mou*, he recognized only now how desperate he'd been back then to stop her retreating from him. His desperation to keep the one good thing in his life amidst the mounting pressure from Theos and the crown. And his own inability to fix the situation between him and Ari. His own inability to handle what she did to him.

He cursed at the color leaching from her face. In a

second, the moment turned from sensual languor to a minefield.

Frustration made his voice rise. "Ariana, you need to share what you're thinking with me."

She nodded, but the wariness was in full force. Her hands around her midriff signaling untouchability. Barriers that he wanted to break but didn't know how. "I just don't want us to chance it. We're not ready."

"Not ready for what?"

"For children, Andreas."

The more she denied him something, the more he wanted to dig in. Andreas wanted to break that harmful pattern of their relationship. Yet something didn't feel right. Something goaded him to provoke her into a reaction. Into an answer. "Sooner or later, we will come to this point."

"It will be later then." Her spine straightened, a combative look in her eyes. "Andreas, we've barely made it through one evening, one, without going at each other's throats.

"I just don't want to bring children into this. At least not yet."

"Why not?"

"Because…between us I don't trust us to get this right."

"You mean, you don't trust me." Frustration coiled up inside him. After everything he had granted her, she still wouldn't give him everything.

Would she ever?

She came to stand in front of him. Lacing her fingers through his, willing him to listen. "It's not that I don't trust you, as much as I…am afraid.

"Please do not force this issue, Andreas."

Again.

The unsaid word hung in the air, morphing and growing like an impenetrable, invisible wall. A thread of disquiet ran through him. A feeling that if he didn't do something, anything, it would always stand between them.

"I want a family. I have always wanted children, you know that."

"You wanted heirs. There's a distinction." Her reply was instant, her eyes saying so much she didn't give voice to.

Feeling as if he was walking through a dark maze blindfolded, an experience his father had forced him through when he'd been eight and confided that he was scared of the dark, he formed and discarded several answers. "The requirement for an heir to the crown is always going to be there, Ariana. Our first child, a boy or a girl, will inherit everything.

"When the Crown Council and Theos put pressure on me to marry these last few years, I considered never doing so. I kept postponing coming to an agreement with Maria's father."

Listening to the other woman's name on his lips sent a shiver through Ariana. "Because of me?"

He shrugged. "I just was not eager to repeat the experience when I thought you were dead. After I found out you were alive…" Ariana had never wished more that she could understand what was going on in his mind. "Nikandros and his children were more than good enough for continuing the House of Drakos.

"So, yes, the heir to the House of Drakos is always going to be a question that will be raised.

"But what I want is…to be a father to my children. To give them the…" She saw him swallow. "The kind of life that I never had."

"What is that?"

"A normal, happy, carefree childhood."

Ariana stood transfixed as emotions buffeted her from all directions.

Guilt and grief choked her breath. Here was the proof that he had truly changed. Just as she had.

Could they make it work this time?

Could she trust that gut instinct of hers that said he cared at least?

She took his hands when he would have moved away. When the small distance she was insisting on could become a chasm neither of them could cross. "I need time. I need it to be just us first. That is, just you and me and Drakon at least."

His gaze probed hers, as if he wanted to know all of her secrets. He lifted their joined hands and kissed her knuckles. The tenderness of the gesture melted her from within.

Lifting his gaze, he held hers. "You've changed," he said finally, his thoughts running parallel to hers.

"I have stopped throwing myself headlong into everything, yes."

He nodded, a set to his jaw. "But I want that old Ariana back. The Ariana that was quick to laugh. The Ariana that loved so generously. The Ariana that lived life to the fullest.

"I assure you, *pethi mou*, I will have that old Ariana back."

CHAPTER TEN

OVER THE NEXT couple of weeks, Ariana found herself more and more captivated by her husband. It was as if he had mounted a campaign to conquer her—mind, body and soul.

And he was winning.

One evening had been a leisurely two hours where they had discussed the red tape she was having to muddle through for her legal agency; one dinner had lasted only an hour and had to be shared with two of his political aides who'd discussed his agenda on his upcoming trip to Asia; once with his PR team and hers, coordinating their schedules and events over the next few months, which had, of course, resulted in a fierce argument between her and Andreas, concerning her duties as the Queen and her increasing devotion to establishing her own career.

Neither of them packed their punches. Neither of them had won.

Ariana had loved every minute of it.

She loved pitting herself against his considerable will. While she never came out the victor, neither did she let him run roughshod over her.

If dinner could not be possible and there had been

days when all she caught was a passing glance of him at a party they were both attending, she found him drifting into the small sitting lounge at precisely ten thirty every night, where she watched an American political satire show, a longstanding favorite of hers.

He would settle down next to her, his hard thigh pressed up against her. Sometimes they laughed at the comedy, sometimes they hotly debated the politics. Sometimes, when they were both far too exhausted, they just fell into a comfortable silence.

But whatever the scenario, a persistent thread of awareness flared between them over the most innocent of contact. Contact, she realized with heat flushing her as she waited for him, she seemed to initiate.

It was she who couldn't keep her hands to herself, who had undone his tie knot one evening when he'd looked utterly flattened after another meeting with the Crown Council, she who had quickly buttoned his shirt, covering that defined chest, when he hadn't quite finished dressing when she and Petra had arrived at the same time one evening, she who had pressed her mouth to his when he had given her his mother's ring.

All he did was watch her from those eyes, the epitome of patience and inscrutability. But Ari knew him as well as she knew herself. Knew that he was waiting for her to make the first move. Knew that it was his kind of foreplay.

He thrived on waiting her out, thrived on pushing them to the edge until every single touch was a fire that could sear.

She didn't know what she was waiting for. She didn't know why she couldn't take that last step in their new relationship. The last time she had jumped into a physical relationship with him, not knowing what was at stake. This time…this time, she knew the value of it.

She knew that when she took Andreas inside her, she would irrevocably lose a part of herself again.

Was it losing her will to his that terrified her?

Or was it the last bit of truth she still held on to?

She wanted nothing between them when he made love to her this time, nothing but want and need.

Except telling Andreas about their son that she had lost terrified her to her core.

They were finally getting to know each other. Finally coming to understand what had gone so terribly wrong the last time. Finally realizing that something akin to magic existed between them. Even out of bed.

"You look utterly serious."

Andreas stood at the entrance to her bedroom. His suit jacket was gone and his white shirt was unbuttoned. The dark shadow of his chest held her attention, her lower body instantly tightening.

She blinked and tried to rearrange her face. "I'm just tired tonight," she replied, realizing it was true. All week, she'd been on conference calls with Magnus and Rhonda and her new lawyer.

He reached the sofa she was sitting on and took a seat without touching her. The tension in his frame radiated out in waves, dismissing her concerns. "Then you need to dial back on the amount of work you're taking on. Petra couldn't find a spare moment from you all of last week."

"Petra needs to stop spying for you," she countered with a smile. Even as his overbearing attitude toward her well-being grated, it also warmed a part of her. For years, she had looked after herself, with no complaints.

But now, she liked that Andreas worried about her. Now she could see his concern for her beneath his arrogant commands.

"Also, will you do the same with your work?" she asked and he grunted. "Very macho, Andreas. Your attitude is beginning to match your communication style."

A long exhale left his lips and he looked at her, a glimmer of a smile around his lips. "You keep up your duties as the Crown Prince's wife, you work all hours setting up your office and dealing with your friends' problems. And yet…"

That he was trying to put this into words rather than railroad her made joy bloom in her chest. "But I'm not being a real wife, am I?" she answered, covering the distance between them.

Dark desire made his eyes glitter. He fingered a wayward curl of her hair and tugged, his mouth a languid curve. "No. One of these days, *agapita*, my patience is going to run out and I'll be inside you and you cannot claim I seduced you.

"I have given you time, Ari." Gravelly and low, his voice pinged over her skin.

Suddenly, she was ready. Just like that.

Before he could blink, she straddled his legs and kissed him.

A long growl erupted from his mouth as he took over the kiss in an instant. Hands on her hips kept her pelvis ground against his, spiking her temperature.

His tongue caressed her with a silky slide, his fingers curling tightly around the nape of her neck.

Ariana moaned loudly when he took her lower lip between his teeth. Threw her head back in a wanton invitation when his hand covered her breast. Drifting her hands down his chest, she covered his groin.

Felt the jolt of his arousal against her palm.

She would have let him take her on the couch right there, if not for the loud peal of her cell phone.

"Ignore it," he growled against her breast.

And it was the command in his voice that made her realize the significance of that ringtone. She slid off him and picked up her phone. And her heart sank.

Andreas somehow managed to dig his senses out of the haze of arousal. Or maybe it was the fast leaching of color from Ari's face that did it.

Ignoring the distress that emanated from her, he wrapped his arms around her while she was still on the call. The lush roundness of her bottom incensed his deprived body a little more. But he liked holding her like that. Even if it was torture.

Somehow, urging his body to calm down, he kneaded the tense jut of her shoulders just as she ended the call.

He knew he wasn't going to like it the second she faced him.

"I have to go," she whispered.

The words sank like stones through his gut. He frowned. Tried to keep his voice even. "Go where?"

"To the States. To Colorado," she said absently, walking circles around the vast room.

"You're not going anywhere," he burst out.

Her awareness jerked back into the room. "Rhonda's divorce came through." Anguish painted her face deathly pale. "Her husband was so pissed off that he hit her. She needs me, Andreas."

Andreas reached for his own phone and called Petra. "I'll have Petra arrange for round-the-clock care for her. And security. That husband of hers won't touch her again."

She was still pale, her body tense. "I should have been there. She was…there for me when I had no one. When it mattered, Andreas," Ariana whispered, as if she hadn't heard a word he'd said.

The very idea made goose bumps rise on his skin. "If you had been there, then you'd have been hurt. *Christos*, Ariana, how could you not share how dangerous your cases are? What if you had been there and he had hit you instead?" Panic made his voice rise, made it harsh. He'd never felt panic like this. He didn't know how to handle it.

Thee mou, was this what came of caring about her?

He never wanted to imagine Ari hurt or worse. "If you want, we'll fly her here as soon as she's able to travel. And first thing tomorrow morning, you'll give over all your case files to Giannis.

"I want a security team vetting every case you take on in the future. You'll be a target as it is without taking on unnecessary—"

Ariana covered his mouth with her hand, her arm going around his body. He stiffened, rejecting her caress, wishing he could reject the answering thrum of his heart as she looked into his eyes.

When had she gained this power over him?

"If you curtail my career, if you do anything to change even the course of it, you'll lose me." Her words were a whisper, an entreaty. As if she understood what she did to him. As if she was willing him to trust this thing between them. Willing him to trust this strange coiling of his own emotions that he was feeling for the first time in his life.

When, suddenly, all he wanted to do was to fight the choke hold of it.

When all he wanted was to have his sterile, uncaring self back.

"It's the same as asking you to walk away from Drakon. Could you do it, Andreas? Could you do it for anything in the world?"

He pulled her hand away from his mouth, his pulse violently ringing in his entire body. "No."

She clasped his cheeks, forcing him to look into her eyes. Forcing him, again, to face what he didn't want to. "Then please trust me. Trust me to do what I need to do. Trust me to keep myself safe. Trust me to come back to you."

Pressing his mouth to the inside of her wrist, he took a deep breath. Letting her go was akin to tearing out a part of him.

But he needed to do it. For both their sakes. To keep a modicum of control over his own emotions.

Whatever madness had consumed his father and whatever manipulations he had run through his children's lives, Theos had been right in one thing.

Emotion was dangerous to men like them, men who held the fates of thousands in the palms of their hands. Men who could abuse that power so easily to rearrange the lives of people closest to them.

Even now, the urge to do something, to ruin her career, her case files, her associations, so that he could keep her safe, so that he could keep her to himself, was so rampant.

My jailer, this time, was the man I loved.

Never again. *Thee mou*, he couldn't do that to her again. He couldn't be the one who killed the spirit inside her.

He let her hand go, and turned away. "Fine, go. I'll give you a week before I'll drag you back here, by your hair if that's what it takes."

He felt her at his back, her arms vined around him, her laughter sending tremors through his frame. "I can't decide if I like you as an academic or a warrior." A wet kiss fluttered near his spine. "I think I like both." Her hands circled to his chest, moved sinuously lower until she was palming his arousal. "I want both."

A deep shudder went through him. Need shook him to the core. "You're a witch." He turned and took her mouth in a punishing kiss. He had to do it. He had to let her go, yet he hated the weakness in his gut. Hated the sweat that gathered at the thought of her not returning.

He poured everything he couldn't say into his kiss. Lifting her off the floor, he plastered her body to his, until even air couldn't separate them. Until she could have little doubt that she was his.

Longing rushed through Ariana, sending little tremors through her body. A haze descended on her and Ari struggled to keep her breathing even.

"Ari? What is it? Ari, are you having an attack?"

"No…" Ari whispered. She could hardly tell him that she was having one of those moments where you realized there was no hope for you.

That something in her was programmed to forever

do what was not good for her. It was like trying to straighten a dog's tail.

"Shh...*agapi mou*. Tell me what I can do, Ari. In this moment, just tell me what you want of me."

"Just..."

Just tell me you love me, please. Tell me so that I can say it back. Tell me so that I can scream it to the world. Tell me so that this time I can truly love you, knowing who you are and knowing who I am.

"You're mine, Ariana. I won't let you go. Anything except that."

Her laughter burst through the tears in her eyes. She had to give him points for constancy. "Just...hold me."

Silently, he tightened his arms around her. His skin was so warm around her, his body lean and yet somehow hard. His heart thundered under her ear as she placed her cheek against his chest. Nothing could equal being held by Andreas. Being dwarfed in his arms, being hit with that sensation of the world righting itself.

At the back of her mind, she was aware everything was changing. She was sinking, falling, and yet she could not stop. She could not be in his life and fight it. She could not be near him and resist what he meant to her. What he'd always meant to her.

She hid her face in his chest, afraid he would see everything in her eyes. "Never let me go," she whispered, shivering.

Three weeks later, coronation day dawned bright and sunny.

Her stomach twisting into a painful knot, her nerves stretched taut, Ariana stared at her reflection in the floor-length mirror in her suite.

The silence was startling after hours of hubbub with designers, hair stylists, her assistants running all over the palace and the palace jeweler, for God's sake.

Only a few minutes before she walked down those curving stairs to a waiting Andreas.

Only a few minutes before the world saw Ariana Drakos.

Only a few minutes before the ceremony that crowned Andreas as King and her Queen.

The gold-edged, oval, floor-length mirror made her dress shimmer as if it had been spun from pure gold.

The bright bulbs overhead made the diamonds in her combs—she'd had to draw the line at the tiara, which had looked more like a crown, and an old, tacky design at that—glitter. The tiny combs, nestled in the complicated up-do she'd twisted her hair into, winked as if there were stars in her hair.

Only now in the first minutes of what seemed like privacy, after hours and hours of makeup artists and stylists and her own secretary hovering over her, did Ariana admit the existence of the football-stadium-sized butterflies in her tummy. Admit to herself that this mattered to her. Far too much.

Of course it did.

It was the moment she had partly run away from. Andreas had given her a reason, yes, but he had also been right.

All Ariana had known then was to run away from difficult situations.

Her father, King Theos, Andreas—they had all been so sure that she'd amount to nothing. Until a few months ago, Ariana had thought she'd never measure up, either.

Had never believed in herself. Had never believed herself worthy of Andreas and everything he had thrust on her in that little fishing village.

Tonight was the culmination of years of sticking to her chosen path, the culmination of the heartache she had suffered, the doubts that had filled her in the darkest moments that her father may have been right, that she was bound to be a train wreck her entire life.

The added layer was that tonight the outer surface matched what she finally believed herself to be inside.

She looked bold, fearless, stylish, a woman who had seduced the ruthless Crown Prince into love. Even she, who had never been into clothes much, had to admit that there was something to be said for the confidence the right designer duds gave.

Her gold ball gown had been a bold choice. Her choice, since Petra and her own secretary likewise thought it unnecessarily defiant. Far too radical.

Ariana didn't give a hoot.

The gold silk was so soft that the soft corset naturally clung to her torso, drawing attention to the meager curves of her breasts. Baring her shoulders, it had a straight neckline and sleeves that fell off her shoulders. At her waist, it flared into a wide skirt.

As she ran a hand over her tummy to calm the butterflies fluttering there, she stilled, stunned by something she hadn't realized until now.

For weeks now, she had tried to shrug off the sinking tentacles of Drakon and all its centuries of glory. Had pretended to scorn the import of today, of her reception by the population of Drakon, to anyone who'd tried to lecture her on the importance of it.

Which meant Eleni, Petra, Andreas's PR team, her own PR team, Nikandros, who thought it hilarious and particularly revelatory when she'd asked him to honestly tell her about the women who'd been running contestants for the coveted role of the future Queen and how she compared against them.

Only Andreas hadn't put that pressure on her since she'd returned—later than the week he'd allotted but in time for the madness that was coronation day.

Only Andreas hadn't filled her head with well-intentioned advice, or warnings, or phrases to be memorized.

Only Andreas had just let her be.

He had not once told her what he expected of her. No questions about if she'd familiarized herself with the Who's Who of the guest list for the ball after, no questions about if she had memorized her statement on her husband's policies about his new directive for the Crown Council.

No comments about sanitizing the reality of the cases she'd dealt with in her everyday life. Cases like Julia's and Rhonda's, cases that rattled some of the most powerful men in the world.

Not even a teasing question about her dress.

Only now, away from the breath-stealing intensity of his gaze, away from that sizzling awareness between them, did she realize that Andreas had showed trust in her abilities, her judgment.

Had he kept his doubts quiet because of their history, or because he actually trusted her to see this through?

Whichever it was, Ariana found she didn't actually care. Did he know what a gift it was that he did not think her unequal to tonight's celebration and fanfare?

Dare she take the risk and tell him the last piece of the past that shimmered between them like a ghost?

The longer she waited to tell him, the harder it was getting. She saw the question in his eyes sometimes. Knew that he didn't like her answer about starting a family. That her lack of trust in him, in them, bothered him.

She did trust him, didn't she? She trusted that he'd changed just as much as she had. That they were both different people now. That any child they might have would be loved by him. In his own way.

Tonight she would tell him. After the coronation, when the frenzy of these few months came to an end. When they could just be Andreas and Ariana again in the intimacy of their bedroom.

She would tell him about the boy they had lost. She would tell him how much she loved him. She had never wanted to so desperately believe her gut instinct. And yet had never been so terrified.

Trembling from head to toe, she turned when she heard someone behind her.

Giannis stood there, his eyes taking her in with a wide smile. "It is time, Your Highness," he said with a nod that acknowledged everything he saw in her eyes.

Head high, Ariana walked to him. On an impulse she couldn't deny, threw herself at him. The good man that he was, Giannis not only caught her but ran a hand over her back comfortingly.

Ariana straightened and nodded, more than grateful for a friend who saw and understood everything.

She was ready for Drakon and its King.

* * *

Ariana realized something was wrong the moment she came down the huge, curving staircase and looked into Andreas's dark eyes.

She faltered on the last step and he caught her. His grip was so tight that she was sure she'd have bruises on her hips from his fingers. A fact he wasn't even aware of, she knew, as his gaze swept over her from head to toe.

Her body rang like a pulse at his slow perusal, at the stark possession in his eyes.

A cold hand fisted her spine.

He knew.

Somehow, he knew what she'd hidden.

"Andreas, I…"

"Did you know that I have been prepared all my life for this moment?" The catch in his throat stunned her, scared her. "To be the King of Drakon, I'd been taught, was my only duty in life. My only purpose.

"And now that the day is here…you have destroyed everything, Ari. Even my belief in myself."

"Andreas…wait, please. How did you know?"

"One of my aides thought it would be a good idea to make sure you had no surprises in your past. The media has a way of getting to those skeletons. And my team always tries to stay two steps ahead of them.

"Imagine the poor man's shock and his nerves when he had to bring that hospital report to me… Can you imagine what you have done to me?"

The next few hours were the most torturous of Ariana's life. Not one of her father's passive-aggressive punishments, not even the pain of premature labor and not knowing if she and the baby would come through, nothing could equal the agony of smiling at people she neither knew nor cared about, when Andreas wouldn't even look at her, nothing could trump the fear that she had, once again, ruined her happiness with her own hands.

But where she normally would have shattered and screamed at the unfairness of it all, she stood ram-rod straight by Andreas's side on the ramparts of the King's Palace and waved at thousands of people lining up the streets of the city.

She never let her smile slip as she accompanied him in an armored car through the streets, never let the tension tying her belly into knots show as they posed for pictures outside the palace.

When she saw Maria Tharius, who seemed to be the very embodiment of poise and patience and every other virtue Ariana didn't possess, and Andreas speaking to each other, his body language utterly relaxed with her, she didn't rant and rave like a lunatic.

The one time she thought she would humiliate herself and the House of Drakos was when they had returned to the ballroom for the first ball given in their honor. When the string quartet began playing and Andreas and she were supposed to open the dancing.

For a few knee-buckling seconds, she thought he would not ask her. Five hundred distinguished guests watching their every interaction like vultures waiting to pick at her flesh. If he didn't ask to dance with her... Nausea rose up.

A harsh exhale left her when he finally uncoupled himself from Maria Tharius and came to stand before her. The perfectly nice smile he had been wearing didn't slip one bit. Only the cold chips of his eyes betrayed his emotions.

The string quartet started a sonata and with a fluid grace she should have expected, he pulled her onto the dance floor. Her heart dipped to her knees and stayed there when he held her as if she were the most precious thing on earth.

Their bodies, which had always fit each other like two puzzle pieces slotting into one, moved in perfect sync. Ariana didn't have to look around to know that they had captured everyone's attention. She wouldn't have to look at the media reports tomorrow to know that the King and Queen of Drakon, unprecedented in the history of Drakon, were madly in love with each other.

When the dance ended and there was a thunderous applause, he pulled her to him and kissed her in complete contrast to the propriety that protocol demanded.

Her heart lurching painfully in her chest, her mouth clinging to his, only Ariana realized what it truly was.

There was no softness, no passion. He punished her with that kiss. Fingers crawling into her sophisticated up-do, he ravished her on the dance floor there. His tongue pushed into her mouth, enslaving her.

Even knowing what he intended, Ariana still clung to him. Her breath hung on a serrated edge, her body teased into painful arousal. Made even more cheap by his poisonous remark against her ear. "Welcome to our future life, my Queen." Color slashed his high cheekbones. "It never fails to amaze me how sweet you taste even when you are filled with the bitterest lies, *agapi mou.* Good thing, too. Because all we have left between us is lies and lust.

"At least conceiving our children should not be as odious a task."

Like jagged thorns, his words pricked Ariana. "What are you talking about?"

A feral gleam erupted in his yes. "I do not give a damn about your timeline, Ari. We will have children and we will have them whenever the mood strikes me.

"Smile, Ariana. You have won over all of Drakon with your perfect act. Someone should benefit from the sordid game you play with our lives."

Swallowing back the tears and the ache from his words, Ariana turned to the guests and smiled. Until her jaw hurt. Until the knot in her throat seemed to cut off the very breath from her lungs.

Andreas was a consummate politician. It was a kiss that generations of Drakonites would talk about.

The romance of a century for their future King and Queen.

The twist that Andreas had wanted to start his reign with had paid off perfectly.

The whole world believed in their love story. And it was in ashes at Ariana's feet.

CHAPTER ELEVEN

It was past midnight by the time Andreas, along with Ariana and his brother and sister, had been able to see off the last guest.

As he'd told Ariana, the evening had been a tremendous success on one measure.

Drakon and the crème de la crème of its society had bought the story of his romance, hook, line and sinker.

They had seen what they had wanted to see—their stoic, emotionless King, made too much in his father's mold, and his beautiful wife with whom he'd irrevocably fallen in love.

It was the stuff of fairy tales, and Drakonites loved their tales more than air.

He had done his duty toward Drakon. More than that, he had given Drakonites something to look forward to after decades of his father's cold, impersonal rule.

Somehow, he'd kept a lid on his exploding temper through it all. No, not somehow. He'd been programmed to behave like this, to put duty to the crown and Drakon above everything else. He'd been programmed until it became a second skin to bury his own emotions, to pretend as if nothing had happened even when he stared at a clinical, cold summary of what his eighteen-year-old wife had suffered.

To find out that she had not only been pregnant when she had left him but that she had almost died delivering his son—his stillborn son—in some godforsaken little village at the foot of the Rocky Mountains with no one around her, it was a picture Andreas could not wipe from his eyes.

And yet, he had carried on like the automaton that he sometimes felt like.

Even Nik and Eleni hadn't suspected anything as he conversed with cabinet ministers and Crown Council members alike.

But now, in the deafening silence of the cavernous palace that had been a prison in so many ways, another chain around his ankles, a sense of utter unreality descended on him. As if something inside him was disconnecting from everything that had always shackled him.

He took the stairs three or four at a time. But there was no running from the very thing that was fracturing inside of him. Propelled by a whirlwind of emotion he had never felt, much less understood, Andreas strode into his suite and came to a standstill.

The massive doors flew back and crashed together at the force with which he had burst them open.

In the gold dress that rippled over every high and dip of that sensuous body, Ariana stood leaning against his vast bed, his downfall and his salvation together in those stricken brown eyes.

As if she belonged in here.

For a minute, all he could do, even now, was stare

at her. Drink her in so that maybe it would keep other ghastly images of her at bay.

She had never looked so breathtakingly beautiful, so poised and perfect as she did tonight.

It was no wonder the media and his very discriminating guests had lapped up the story they had been fed. With that mystifying combination of confidence and innocence, strength and vulnerability, Ariana made it very easy to buy that any man, even he whose heart was made of stone, would tumble recklessly into love with her.

That any man would defy conventions and propriety to own her. And it was not just how she had looked today. It was how she had engaged people. No amount of coaching or being prepped by his team of aides would have made her look more like the genuine article.

Would have made her speak up with more passion about serving the people. About joining her husband in seeing to it that Drakon emerged victorious again after the last decade in a funk.

Against all odds, it was clear that Ariana had finally accepted Drakon. That she had finally come into her own for the role he'd always wanted her in.

She had become everything Theos had wanted in the future Queen.

She'd almost died, something inside him screamed again. It was as if the loss that had nearly destroyed him when he'd returned from the oil summit, he'd have to live through it again.

His brain provided vivid images of her pale and unconscious lying in some wretched hospital, surrounded by strangers.

Afraid and alone, yet determined to not return to him at any cost. Consigning him to a life of loneliness, destroying the little joy she had brought him.

"Get out of my suite."

"I'm not going anywhere." Defiance and something else screamed from every angle of her body. "Never again. I…" She looked away and then back at up him again. "I was going to tell you today. It's been killing me to hold it inside. Please, believe me that I was going to tell you today."

"Your words mean nothing to me anymore."

The intensity of the fury building inside him, the jagged edge of betrayal, threatened to take him out at his knees.

Was this what he had dreaded ten years ago? Had he always known that she would reduce him to this—the lowest denominator of himself—that his father had worked hard to beat out of him? Had Theos known that Ariana would have the power to bring him to his knees like this?

Her hands went around her midriff, her body faintly swaying from side to side. "No. I want to discuss this."

Ignoring her, he walked toward his closet and she blocked him. Like a drug addict, he pulled the scent of her skin deep into his lungs.

"Get out of my way, Ariana."

She stood in front of him, tension radiating out of every pore.

"If you don't move out of my way, I will not be responsible for what I do."

"I'm not afraid of you, Andreas. I was afraid of what… I became around you, of what our lives would become if I stayed. I was immature, reckless."

"Nothing you say or do today is going to change the way I feel."

A jagged laugh fell from her mouth, far too close to the sound a cornered animal would make in its last bid for freedom. "If only I had known that this last piece of bitter truth was what I needed to spill to get you to talk about your feelings, then I would have done so a long time ago."

Rage clawing through him like a tsunami, Andreas backed her into the wall until she was caged by his body against it. "What the hell is wrong with you that you would joke about such a thing? How dare you mock me about hiding the fact that you had my son and nearly—" his throat felt like there were pieces of glass in there "—died in the process?"

Finally, she must have seen something of what he was feeling in his eyes for her brown eyes widened. And even that lasted only a few seconds before she tilted her chin up and looked him square in the eye. "I lived through that, Andreas. I know what I suffered." Tears filled her eyes and ran down her cheeks. "The guilt that something in me made that happen, the grief that drowned me for months...they will not leave me in this lifetime."

She ran the back of her hands over her cheeks roughly and swallowed. "I'm not defending my decision making at that time. I was—"

"A pathological liar? A woman incapable of thinking maturely?"

"By the time I found out that I was pregnant, you were already engaged to another woman. Think this through, I had already signed papers agreeing to dissolve our marriage.

"If I had come back, if I had told you back then that I was pregnant, you would have made my life miserable as hell. Loving you with nothing in return was already half killing me.

"The fact that I even got pregnant when it was the last thing we needed in our lives is not my fault. The fact that you thought bringing a child into a...rocky relationship would fix everything...that was your fault."

Every word out of her mouth was truth that raked its claws through him. "I asked you to get off the pill because it was the only other way I could convince Theos to accept you. I knew, in the back of my mind, what he was doing to you. I saw the stricken look in your eyes, I saw how subdued you were becoming. I thought I was losing you.

"If you became pregnant, then I could convince him. Then we could give each other a chance..."

Shock made her lips flatten. Hard. "So my choice was to lose myself or to become your broodmare?"

"At the time, you were good for nothing else, so yes. If I wanted to keep you in my life, those were my choices."

She flinched at his words but he didn't care. God, nothing mattered except that he hurt her back as she had hurt him. Nothing mattered except to assuage the pain ripping him open inside.

Even caged against him, she was not feeble. Not fragile. Something glowed in her face, as if there was a light in her again. As if she was that girl who could conquer anything with her very will to live. With her laughter. "How about the simple reason that you loved me just as I was? That you needed me in your life, just as I was? How about standing up to the mighty King

Theos and telling him that you were so desperately in love with me that you couldn't go on without me?

"That despite his every cruel treatment, despite his every effort to make you into stone, you still felt so much for me. That you...you loved me and it made you so off balance, so disconcerted that you immediately tried to push me away when we returned?

"That you're, after all, human, Andreas."

Bitterness was a rock in her throat. A jagged-edged one. She was truly lost if she thought he had loved her. "*Christos*, I ruined your life, Ari. Isn't that what you've been trying to tell me for weeks now?

"If you want to call it love, then you're as screwed up as I'm, *glykia mou*. Do you not see that?"

"I loved you so much and your incapability to handle what you felt for me...your inability to accept it for what it was, that's what drove me away. That's what terrified me about coming back.

"The fate of becoming my own mother again... dying inside a little every day."

Andreas turned away from her, just the act of breathing hurting his lungs.

Did it drill down to that as he'd always known, always feared? Did it come down to the fact that even now, he could not process or admit to his own feelings?

She pressed against his back, her body trembling. "I was afraid of what you and your father would do to our child. I was afraid that if I came back to you, you would..."

He turned with a vicious snarl. *Dios*, he just couldn't take anymore. But she was determined to rip him up, she was determined to prove that there was something in him worth loving. "We would do what?"

"I was terrified that King Theos and you would repeat history. That it would be another person your father would control. I was terrified that you would turn our son into…another you. That like my own mother, I would have no say in the bringing up of our child. I stayed away for the baby, Andreas."

The bare truth of her words fragmented the last thread of his self-possession.

He crushed his mouth to hers, for he couldn't stave off that fear spreading through him. Couldn't find a way to hold off the anger, the desperation and worst of all that hurt that seemed to saw through him.

She was right. Theos had made him into this and there was nothing he could do. He could not love her. He still had nothing to offer her.

All the rage he felt at himself, his father and Ariana mutated into this raw, overwhelming need to possess her, the only time in his entire life when he felt something.

The only thing in his life he still had, the only thing that was real and constant in his tilting world.

He poured everything he had ever felt into that one kiss, dragging his mouth over hers desperately. As if she was air and he would expire if he let go of her.

Her mouth was sweet and soft, a cavern of welcoming heat. A place where he'd always found something he didn't know he was missing.

"Andreas, please—"

A sob burst out of her mouth when he buried his hands in her hair and tugged roughly. He had no control anymore and he didn't give a damn. He tangled his tongue with hers, licking in and out of her mouth. The more he kissed her, the more he wanted.

In some portion of his mind, he was aware that she was trying to talk. That she had more to say. But he didn't want to hear any more. He didn't want excuses. He didn't want more accusations even though he knew most of what she said was true. He wanted nothing but to drown himself in sensation.

So he took her mouth again and again, rough and hard.

He bit her lip when she tried to argue.

He licked at that nip when she sobbed.

He thrust his tongue into her mouth when she moaned.

He molded her body with his hands when she thrashed against him.

At some point, she had stopped trying to get him to listen and began giving as good as she got. Slim hands were clutching him, pushing back his suit jacket. Nails digging into his nape. Fingertips gripping his buttocks.

He laughed against her mouth, a bitter, twisted sound. He'd forgotten how much she loved his body. How many hours she'd spent kissing and licking him. Testing and teasing. Theos's excruciatingly rigorous physical regimen had come in handy in this.

Desire banishing any sense, he picked her up and ate up the few strides to his enormous bed. The French doors were open, he could hear the whisper of the staff walking back and forth across the courtyard. But he didn't care.

All he needed was to be inside her.

He devoured her and she devoured him, their focus so completely on each other that the outside world melted.

"Andreas…you didn't let me finish. Please, let me—"

His questing hands found the zipper of her dress and half pulled, half tore it away from her pliant body. Bra undone, her breasts spilled against his hands. The tips engorged when he ran his knuckles over the nipples. He pushed her onto the bed and her hair billowed on his pristine white sheets like burnished copper.

A string of silk was the only thing that separated him from the warmth he needed. From the moment Theos had let it slip that she was alive, he'd needed this. Only with her had he ever been like this. An animal that let instinct rather than reason drive him. Years' worth of need burst through him like water through a dam.

He saw so many things in her body. So many things she'd given him with her generosity and all he'd done...

Only staring at her gorgeous body held off the pain. The ache of how much they'd lost. The fear...the stabbing fear that he was still that same man.

That he would only destroy her again.

With his palm splayed on her lower back, he pushed her onto the bed.

He ripped off the flimsy piece of silk from her body. Dizzying need. Glorious freedom.

The taut curves of her buttocks. The neat little indentation of her waist. The fluid arc of her spine. The long, trembling muscles of her thighs. The toned arms that she had spread under her. The fingers digging into the silky sheets for purchase.

He let his gaze rove up and down her body like a starved man staring at a feast. Goose bumps were rising on her skin, exposed suddenly to the cold air.

There was no mercy in him tonight.

She laid her head on one cheek, her shallow breaths

making the air near her head fly in a mesmerizing rhythm. Their eyes met and held. There were tears in her eyes, unspilled, making them huge in that gamine face. Her already pouty lips were swollen and a voluptuous pink.

He might as well have been a predator holding down prey for the continual shudders that coursed through her body.

Exposed to him like this, she should have looked feeble. At least fragile. Yet there was a fire in her eyes that dared him to take her like that. To continue on the explosive path he seemed to have pushed them to, even as she quivered like a finely tuned string under the softest of his touches.

"*S'agapo*, Andreas. So much. Always." *I love you, Andreas.*

The words seared him like lashes against bare skin. Like lightning striking things to ground. Like hot spewing lava burning up everything in sight.

The true meaning of those words terrified him, bound him when all he'd wanted was to walk away.

Just once, he promised himself. He would take her for this one night. He would let himself revel in those words this one time.

Holding her gaze like that, he unzipped his trousers and pushed them and his boxers down. His erection sprang free and he saw the tiniest flicker of something—hunger, fear, he didn't care what the hell it was—in her eyes. Heard her breath quicken.

His arousal lengthened at the greed in her eyes. With a growl he couldn't contain, he shed his shirt and undershirt. "Spread your legs, *agapi mou*," he whispered and she complied like a nice, docile wife.

Legs straddling hers, he bent his body over hers. The skin-to-skin contact sent heat ripping between them. She was like spun silk against his rough chest. Her buttocks an inviting cradle for his rock-hard flesh. When she tried to move against him, he locked her movements with his hands on her wrists, using a bit of his own superior strength against hers.

Sounds ripped out of their mouths in unison, a hoarse symphony of need and desire. Sensations they had both long forgotten shimmered close. Fluttered in and out in their harsh breaths as their bodies recognized things their minds hadn't.

God, he loved her like this. He needed this submission from the woman who constantly defied him, who again and again set his world upside down. He needed her willing and wanton beneath him because it was the only place where there was complete honesty between them.

Where she couldn't hide anything more from him.

Where she couldn't retreat behind lies.

Where he was enough for her.

He dug his teeth into her upper shoulder. She bucked under him, thrusting into his hardness with a sob. "More, Andreas. Everything you can give."

The sheets whispered and slithered around them as he grazed a few more spots on her lovely back. He licked the tender spots, already bruising. Sensual and all woman, her taste licked through his veins, incinerating.

His erection caught between their bodies was like velvet-encased steel.

She was moaning and clawing at the sheets when he slipped his hand between her legs. Her slick warmth was like molten fire over his fingers. He felt her writhe under him, trying to arch her pelvis into his hand, searching mindlessly for the rhythm that would bring relief.

He stroked her long and leisurely, opened her up and sank his fingers into her, never giving her the pace she wanted. Stringing her along until she was one long pulse of sensation underneath him.

In a flash of movement, she turned under him, until she was facing him. "Don't retreat from me, please. Andreas. Don't treat me as if I'm nothing but a body to you."

"But you're just that, Ariana. I can give you nothing but this. I have never given you anything but this, *agapi mou*. When will you learn?"

"No, no, no," she said, thrashing against him. Bringing her body flush against his, she brought her mouth to his in a crushing kiss. Her breasts were crushed against his arm, her legs tangled with his. She kissed as if she meant to hold him to her with it.

"I was wrong," she whispered against his mouth, pressing kisses all over his face. "We are both different now, Andreas. We have a chance and I will not—"

He slammed his mouth against hers. Kicking her legs apart, holding her with his hands on her hips, he entered her welcoming warmth with one deep stroke. No warning, no waiting.

A groan ripped from his throat. Her snug sheath closed around his hardness like a glove.

Like they'd never been apart. As if in this moment, in this place, they were not two but one.

Anchoring her with one arm, he palmed her breast with another. The tip was an erotic contrast surrounded by the lush softness. Pleasure coiled and corkscrewed in his groin, and shivered down his spine. Lost to the demands of his own body, he pulled out and thrust back in slow, hard thrusts that had her silky body sliding up against the sheets.

Sensation spiraled through him, erasing the grief and guilt and betrayal, the only thing that could wash away the powerlessness he felt.

Mouth buried in her neck, he slammed in and out, branding her, making her his in every way. She was perfect under him, around him, the one woman who had always made him feel that he was not alone. That made him dream that he did not have to be alone.

S'agapo, *Andreas. So much. Always.*

The words mocked him, taunted him. Charged the moment with so much more than the pure carnality of it all.

He wrapped his hand around her neck, and pulled her up, until on each thrust in, her sex felt him. All of him. He increased the pace just as her body was tensing up around him. Her muscles clenched and released around his hardness, her body bucking and throwing. She orgasmed with a soft moan, her eyes open and holding his, daring him—oh, how they dared him—always to make nothing of this moment.

It was the fire in her eyes that pushed Andreas over the edge. Lost to desire, he plunged into her with hard, rough, desperate strokes.

His climax was violent, explosive, moving through him like a storm he would never survive. This connection between them had always made everything worth it. Had somehow made sense of everything else.

Heart pounding inside his chest, he stilled. Loath to

give up her warmth, he stayed inside, swallowing away the aftershocks of her orgasm still rocking through her.

Sweat-dampened, her skin glistened and invited. Her mouth looked like it had been stung by bees. Faint bruises on her hips showed where he had held her down while he had thrust into her.

Long lashes flickered up slowly. The musky scent of their sweat and sex filled his nostrils.

He couldn't walk away, even though it was exactly what he'd intended to do. Still intended to do.

CHAPTER TWELVE

WHEN ARIANA WOKE up the first time, morning had come. Even through the light-blocking blinds, she could see the world outside had started on its day. Every inch of her body was sore in the most glorious way. A muscular, hair-dusted leg lay possessively over hers, hindering her movement. The oversize T-shirt she wore bunched up to her midriff thanks to the arm curled around her waist holding her caged against the hard muscles behind.

She tried to shift to a more comfortable position and gasped at the unfamiliar sting between her thighs.

The night before came back in a rush. Instinctively, her gaze fell on the darkly handsome face sharing the pillow. His other arm was under her head, his biceps muscles curling tight. Faint shadows under his eyes, even in sleep, Andreas looked like he had the weight of the world on his shoulders.

Or was it the weight of her lies?

Had she lost him forever this time?

Only now, when it was too late, did she realize the destruction she had caused with her secrets and her cowardice.

But the stinging throb between her legs, the faint

bruises on her body said something else. She had been terrified that he would throw her out. Or walk away.

Last night, she knew, was the first time Andreas Drakos had ever lost complete control of himself. There had been no finesse to his lovemaking. *Thee mou*, it hadn't even been lovemaking. It had been sex in its most primitive form. It had been pure possession, as if he meant to steal something away from her.

It had been his incapability to walk away from her even at the worst moment of their lives.

The rough graze of his teeth over the most tender spots of her body, the flash of emotions, too fast for her to even notice, in his eyes. The frantic, animalistic thrusts, uncaring of whether he hurt her. Ariana reveled in every ache and pain that her body sang this morning.

She had wanted, desperately needed, every sensation he'd evoked in her.

She had loved every minute of it.

For it meant that she could still hold on to a thread of hope. That meant that despite what he thought was the biggest betrayal, Andreas still couldn't help himself.

He had carried her to the shower, she remembered faintly. While she had stood there numb, her body sore, he had washed her, wrapped her in a towel and brought her back to bed. Dressed her in his T-shirt.

When she had thought he would leave her, she had clung to him, she remembered now, even her subconscious mind knowing that to let him walk away then was to lose him. She had begged him to stay with her, at least until she had fallen asleep. She had begged him to give her one night.

His dark hair fell onto his forehead. He needed a shave and sleep and rest in that order. God, Andreas needed to be loved. Needed to be showed that he could love, too.

She ran her fingers over the defined line of his jaw, the sharp bridge of his nose. Her fingers shook at the soft give of his mouth. The scent of sex and him lingered in the air, an anchor Ariana needed in the chaos she had created.

Anxiety curling through her, she ran her hands over warm, olive skin stretched taut over lean muscles. Every inch of him was precious to her. Every inch of him was a map to her own happiness, to her joy.

She pressed her mouth to his chest, listening to the quiet thunder of his heart. She began to whisper words and phrases that made no sense yet meant everything to her. Things she should have told him before about her life in Colorado. Times when she had missed him so terribly that it had been a physical ache.

Nights when she'd craved his arms, even in the last few weeks.

Moments during the past week when all she'd wanted was to walk into his bedroom and climb into his bed. When all she'd needed was to be held in his arms.

At some point, the words had begun to tumble out without any conscious plan. His body lost that languid sleepy warmth. Tension filled the very air, the quiet hitch in his breath the only sign that her words had begun to register. Without meeting his eyes, for Ari was terrified he would walk away the moment she acknowledged him, she kept talking. The dark helped. The physical intimacy aided. Running her hands again and again over him kept her sane, as if touch were her only tether to keep him there.

She was on her side, and he on his, facing her. She spoke the words into his chest, words she should have uttered the moment she'd seen him standing in front of the church.

The moment she'd realized that without Andreas, she would always be incomplete.

She didn't know if he was listening. She just kept talking, her throat hoarse, her body sore. "By the time I realized my period was far too late, even worse than usual, I was three months pregnant. I... I took four different tests, and they all came back positive." He was so tense around her, suddenly so cold. As if someone had injected him with ice. She rubbed his arms and his chest with her palms, her tummy a tight knot. Expecting him to any moment push her away. "I...should have been terrified and yet I was not. I know you will call it another sign that I was immature and juvenile, but I wasn't. I felt an instant connection to the baby. I...felt like finally I had a part of you with me. Just for me. Something no one could take away from me. Not even you.

"I...had already found an apartment. Until then, I'd proudly refused to use the money Theos gave me. But that night, I went into the bank, checked my account.

"For months all I did was eat, sleep, wait. I was determined to take good care of myself. I...put on so much weight," she said, her throat catching at the memory.

"Everything was perfect until one afternoon it wasn't.

"Rhonda drove me to the hospital because pains had started and showed no signs of relenting.

"I was knocked out by the drugs and when I finally woke up…" her tears soaked Andreas's chest. Her throat burned. Her lungs felt as if they were being crushed. "I screamed at the doctor, demanding to know who had decided that my life was more precious than his.

"I was hysterical.

"They told me he'd never had a chance. I insisted on seeing him and fell apart at the sight of that tiny bundle."

Soft sobs began to shake through her body and Ariana could no more stop them than she could stop breathing. Andreas's arm came over her and crushed her to his chest. He held her hard and tight, in an almost bruising grip. The heat from his body was a blanket over her, warm and comforting.

It was exactly what she'd needed for so long. This grief, it was his, too. And she had cheated him out of it, because she had been so…afraid of never being loved in return.

"Shh…*agapi mou*," he finally said. Shaken and hoarse, as if he had damaged his throat, too. She felt his fingers move through her hair, his mouth breathing the words into her temple. "I would have made the same choice if it had come to that, Ari. I would have chosen your life…"

"I did everything right, Andreas," she said, needing to tell him this. Needing his forgiveness in this above everything else. "I was careful. I ate well. I took walks. I slept well. I went in to see the doctor for every twinge and ache. I… But I still failed at protecting him. I… never wanted to—"

His fingers were now digging into her arms, but

holding her together, too. "Ariana, listen to me. He was…he was not meant to be. But it is not your fault, do you understand? All the things I said about you being reckless… I can comprehend how much you must have loved…that baby. I know how you love, *agapi mou*."

Ariana lifted her gaze, her heart beating rapidly in her chest. Grief made the planes of his face harsher, even more stark. He ran the pad of his finger against her cheek, hesitant. Naked emotion fluttered in his eyes, for the first time since she had known him. "You… How long were you out for?"

He had been so afraid for her last night, she realized now. She saw the nightmare of it in his frenzied movements, in his shattered self-control. The words in that clinical report had been enough for him to imagine what she had been through. "Two days. They said I had lost too much blood."

He nodded, a far-off look in his eyes. A look she knew very well. His detachment look. His "burying away emotion because he didn't know what to do with it" look.

His retreat look.

"After they discharged me, after I came back to my apartment, one evening I sat with the phone in my hand, my fingers hovering over the numbers. I… had never felt so alone in the world. Not even when they came to our house and told me that my parents' car had crashed.

"I…desperately wanted to see you, wanted to be held by you. To just give myself over. To let you mold me into whatever you needed me to be. Anything felt better than what I had done with my life."

"Why didn't you? *Thee mou*, Ariana, why did you not call me? Had you no trust in me at all?"

"There was nothing good left by then. Everything was in ashes and I... I realized I had to move on. I had to make sense of my life. I had to change how I lived it.

"I always used my father's rejection of me as motivation to ruin my life. To do as I pleased. I realized... I was just proving him right. I decided that night that I wouldn't let him be right.

"The next morning, Rhonda got me a job at the agency. And I never looked back."

"I saw it in your eyes the first moment I laid eyes on you. I knew immediately you had changed."

Ariana nodded, dismay coiling up at how...unangry he sounded. So much like the normal Andreas. As if he had gone through the entire range of emotion from fury to grief and was now back to his default state of feeling nothing. "I think a part of me died with our son. I...never wanted to love like that again. I didn't want that pain again. I thought..."

She cupped his face in her hands, desperate to make him understand. "Andreas, when you found me standing at the church, I... I was about to call Magnus. I was about to call it off."

His dark eyes held hers. Wariness and something else she couldn't even identify. "Call what off?"

"The wedding. I realized I just couldn't go through with it. After everything I thought needed to change in me, it seemed nothing had changed where it mattered. I knew you were going to announce your alliance with... You were going to announce your choice for a wife.

"You...would be King and have a new Queen.

"Whether you knew it or not, whether you were in my life or not, it didn't matter. You still had a part of me. You still had possession of my heart after all those years." She felt the tension that rippled through his hard body. Every inch of him screamed rejection. Every inch of him wanted to walk away.

The very instinctual gesture sent deep shivers of fear through her.

He had always wanted her love. Thrived on it. Even a week ago, he'd challenged that he would win it back.

All she was now was an emptiness in his eyes. A resignation that was clawing through her. "I…realized the happy, safe, grown-up life I thought I had with a nice man… I just didn't want it, after all. That you had ruined me for any other man."

"Ariana…" A warning.

She pressed her finger against his lips, desperate for the right words. "I was not ready to admit it to you when you showed up. I wasn't ready to admit it to myself, but I… I never stopped loving you.

"I love you, Andreas.

"I have always loved you. I just… I needed to be worthy of you. Worthy of standing by your side, to rule Drakon. I needed to be more than the train wreck my father thought I was before I could truly understand the meaning of loving you."

The moment stretched, his silence deafeningly heavy in the wake of her words. It was as if she was trying to hold on to this moment between them, trying to freeze time, and it insisted on getting away from her.

"Andreas…please say something. Curse me. Rage at me."

Turning away from her, he pulled up on the bed.

Face buried in his hands, he exhaled roughly. "What we have, this, is never going to be enough, Ariana. We might as well accept it.

"The choice is yours."

Fear was a bitter taste on her tongue. "What choice?"

"Whether you want to stay with me or not." Black eyes became opaque pools, reflecting nothing. As if there was nothing. He took her hand in his, traced the veins on the inside of her wrist. As if he was asking her out to dinner while in reality, he was shredding her to pieces.

Rising to her knees, Ari pleaded with him. "Punish me all you want, Andreas, but please give me a chance. Give me a chance to prove that you can forgive me."

"Punish you? Forgive you?" He shook his head. The bleakness in his eyes made nausea rise up in her throat. "Do you still not see, Ari? Do you not see how much we've lost, how much we... Every time I close my eyes, *I see you*. Lying on some stretcher, pale, out of it. Alone. I drove you to that.

"Even if I forgive you, I cannot forgive myself.

"Even if I trust you, I can't trust myself. To not destroy you all over again."

The shudder that went through his powerful frame sent Ariana through a spiral of desperation. "You've changed," she whispered, her voice husky and rough from all the screaming. "I've changed. We have walked through fire, Andreas. And we have both come out strong."

She traced the angles of his face with shaking fingers. Wet, warm, open-mouthed kisses, she spread them over his torso as if she were sprinkling her own brand of fairy dust.

As if she could somehow make him believe that he could love her, too.

Hands fisted by his sides, he closed his eyes. His breath became harsh, falling on her like soft strokes. She pulled away the duvet that was tangled around their legs and straddled him.

Sinking her hands into his hair, she kissed his temple, his eyes and finally his mouth. He didn't move, he didn't react.

A sob rising through her, Ariana dug her teeth into his lip. Moved her mouth down his throat, licked the velvet rough skin of his shoulder. "You love me, Andreas. I will believe it enough for both of us, until you do. You love me, you love me, God, I was such a fool to not see it then. I was such a fool to not stand and fight for you." She whispered into his skin, the love she felt for him overflowing out of her.

Pushing onto her knees, she pulled off the oversized T-shirt he'd put on her. Arms wrapped around his back, she vined herself around him. His chest crushed her breasts, the angular ridge of his hips digging roughly into her inner thighs.

And then she kissed him. Softly, slowly, stroking and tracing every inch of his sculpted mouth. Pouring everything she felt for him into that kiss.

Only then did he open his eyes. Dark color slashed his cheekbones, his breath out of rhythm. His hands descended to her hips and spread her open, wicked desire glinting in his eyes.

Her breath hitched. Every particle in her stilled as he delved his fingers into her slick flesh. "This proves nothing, Ari. You were right. You have always been my weakness." One finger and then two penetrated her sensitive flesh. He licked circles around her nipple, never touching the tip.

Making her crazy for more. "You want to be a part of my life? *Kala.* You want me to continue—" his mouth closed over her nipple and he suckled so deeply that Ariana rocked her pelvis into his washboard stomach "—giving you this mindless pleasure that is the only real thing between us, *kala.* I'm more than happy to, but that's all it is, Ari.

"Your destruction, *agapita*, will not be at my hands this time."

Sensations spiraled through her. Her spine arched, and Ariana tried to hold on to her thoughts. To not give in to the riot of pleasure that forked through her lower belly. Breathing hard, she stilled his fingers wreaking havoc inside her sex. Just the way he knew would drive her over the edge. "You came for me. After everything I did, you still came for me. You searched for me for two years. That counts—"

His thumb pressed at her clit in erotic circles. Daring her to continue. Drowning her in delirious sensation. Sweat beaded on her skin. All rationality was lost again.

The second he rubbed the thick head of his erection against her swollen flesh, Ariana screamed. Tears gathered in her eyes but there was no turning off the kaleidoscope of sensations arrowing down her lower belly.

"This is all I can give you. This and the status and the respect that I would give any woman I'd have married. I would not cheat on you, but I would not love you, either.

"I will not care what you do with your life, you

could learn cabaret for all I care, but I would not love you."

Ariana bit her lip hard, wondering if actual physical pain could arrest the climax building through her.

"But—"

Holding her gaze, he wrapped his fingers over her buttocks, lifted her and then sank her down onto his rock-hard flesh. So fully and completely. It stung first and then fire spread through her muscles. He pushed up into a sitting position, his thighs pressing hers inward, one hand locking her wrists.

His mouth buried between her breasts, his voice ragged. "Move, Ari. Move as your body wants you to, *pethi mou*." His eyes closed as her body did its own instinctual, age-old thing to relieve the ache there. "This I will give you, Ariana." With that promise, he took her nipple in his mouth, wrapped his tongue around it.

There was no way to control her body's response. Ariana moved up and down sending guttural groans out of their mouths. His hips surged up, cleaving through her, his eyes glittering in the dark. Stark possession shone in them. "We should not have ever come together, Ari. I…should have never married you."

Tears streaming down her cheeks, her body racing toward the peak, Ari bent down and kissed him softly. "I will choose to believe it was love that brought you to me.

"I will believe for the rest of our lives if that's what it takes. I will be here day and night. Waiting for you. And wanting you."

She repeated the words again and again as pleasure skewered through her body and he covered it with his own, chasing his own climax. He filled her completely, utterly.

And yet Ariana had never known such loss.

When she woke up again, among cool sheets, sticky and sore between her legs, he was gone. The huge room was dappled in afternoon light, bright and pricking her eyes. She didn't have to get up and ask his secretary to confirm what she already knew.

He would have already left the King's Palace.

CHAPTER THIRTEEN

ARIANA HAD FORGOTTEN. Or had she given up counting the number of days since Andreas had left the King's Palace? After the third day, nights and days began to merge.

There were no tears this time. She hadn't ranted and raged after he had walked out.

She lost herself in studying for the bar exam. In developing the contacts she'd made at the ball that would aid in her starting her own legal agency. Under Petra and Giannis's expert guidance, she gave an interview about the work she was going to take up once she was licensed to practice law in Drakon.

She visited two different organizations in the city, who provided relief and shelter to abused women, and came up with action items to tackle the poorly funded shelters. Eleni, she was slowly realizing, was a veritable mine of information on the topic of fund-raisers and charity auctions.

Taking her advice on board, Ariana threw herself into organizing her fund-raiser.

She worked from sunup to sundown, trying to exhaust herself. But when her head hit the pillow in that big king bed of Andreas's, sleep still eluded her frantic mind.

If Ariana had thought him unapproachable before, he was nothing short of the arctic freeze now.

He was utterly polite to her. He constantly checked with her to make sure she had everything she needed to realize her own dream. He respected her opinion, he even let her accompany him on a short trip to some of the key rural areas where Gabriel's firm was investing in the economy by building world-class resorts.

He treated her like he would have treated any other woman he could have married. With the utmost civility. As if she were a complete stranger he was sharing his life with. As if there was no more to him than the perfect ruler, or the polite husband.

The worst part was that Ariana had no idea if he was doing it to distance himself from her, or if he truly felt nothing. The probability that she had lost him this time…had robbed her of a single night's peaceful sleep.

After the first three weeks of being simply stonewalled, she'd lost her patience one night. Clearly, giving him space and time wasn't working.

Nothing, it seemed, was working.

In an attempt to talk to him, to confront him, she had crawled into his bed one night, knowing that he'd returned at midnight from another trip. After waiting for hours, she had finally fallen into a restless sleep. She had woken up to realize it was his mouth on her neck, his hands on her legs that had hurtled her out of sleep.

He'd hardly even greeted her before he covered her mouth with his. He gave her hardly a chance to breathe when he pushed her legs apart, rid her of her panties and pressed his mouth to her sex.

Ariana didn't remember how many times he'd made her climax that night before he had pushed her face down, spread her legs and taken her from behind. He had exhausted her so deeply that her bones had been jelly, her entire body so sensitive and sore that finally she had fallen into a deep sleep.

When she'd awoken, showered and dressed on buckling knees, he had been gone again.

The pattern continued for two months. Every time he went on a trip, he stayed away for longer. He sent her the most exotic, expensive gifts. He barely even met her eyes anymore. If he found her in his bed, he made love to her. If she wasn't there, he didn't seek her out.

Sometimes they barely got their clothes off, he was that desperate and rough. Sometimes, he made love to her with soft, soothing words. So tenderly, as if she was the most precious thing he had ever beheld. As if he couldn't help himself.

Nikandros and Mia, Eleni and Gabriel had even stopped inquiring about what was wrong. Said only that she looked like a wraith and that Andreas was… well, more unapproachable than ever. She heard the staff, even Petra, who was as loyal as they came, say that he was even more unforgiving than before. That anyone who made one mistake, one misstep with him, got their head chewed off. While to the outside world, they couldn't be happier and more in love. More perfect for each other.

And slowly Ari began to lose hope.

The whole palace was in a mad rush because Eleni had gone into labor all of a sudden.

Ariana had wrapped the little booties and sweater

she had knitted in soft tissue paper, eager to visit the little infant, when she heard two aides talking.

Andreas was returning tomorrow, was cutting his trip short to see Eleni's little girl. Eleni had already told Ariana that she wanted Ariana and Andreas to be their little one's godparents.

When Ariana had argued they were the last couple who knew anything about babies, Eleni had shook her head and said she trusted her little girl with the both of them.

As always, Ari's heart thundered at the thought of his return. Longing twisted through her, entangled with hope that, this time, things would be different. That this, the distance, would have been enough for him to see she was here. And that she had no thought of leaving him.

Slowly, as if someone was siphoning away life from her, she lost steam. Coming to rest against a dark mahogany door, she tried to catch her breath past the glass in her throat.

Was she just deluding herself?

He would smile and nod at her with those dark eyes. Tell Eleni that she would make the perfect godmother. Then walk away, especially because this was about a child.

A matter that would always be raw and guilt-ridden between them. A matter it seemed he could not get over.

Then, if she was fortunate, he might come to bed. And if he did, and Ariana tried to talk, he would make love to her until she forgot her own name.

Come morning, all she'd have was a sore body and a crushed heart.

Maybe he was right. Maybe things between them were so broken that they could not be fixed again. But *Thee mou*, she could not live like this.

She couldn't be near him and love him and live day after day knowing that he might never accept his love for her. This was even worse than what she'd run away from. She couldn't bear this…any longer.

Tired and beaten down, all she wanted was to run away. To escape.

But she couldn't. Andreas hadn't given up on her in ten years and she hugged the fact to herself.

She wiped her palms over her mouth, instructed one of the staff to give her present to Eleni and then went back to her suite. Dismissing everybody else, she took Giannis into confidence, told him how to reach her in an emergency.

Like Andreas raising a palace-wide search for her. But no, she was sure he would hardly even notice for a month or two.

She packed a small bag personally, throwing in just enough necessities. Had a car brought round to her, got into the driver's seat and drove away.

She was not running away, she told herself. She was playing the only card she had left to win him over.

Andreas walked away from Eleni's suite, his gut a hard coil of twisting emotions. His new niece, Maria Drakos Marquez, had fit into half his forearm.

She had smelled like baby powder, and new life, and utter joy.

Her eyes glittering like Gabriel's, her mouth stubborn like her mother's, she had been the most absolutely precious thing Andreas had ever beheld.

The infant's little smile felt as if it had clawed into his chest and thumped his heart into a thunderous roar.

His vision had shimmered so dangerously for a second that he had quickly given her over to Nikandros, who was a proud and wonderful dad to his twins.

All he'd been able to see for a few seconds had been another child. With dark hair, and dark eyes like his, as Ariana had told him.

A boy, his son.

His heart thumped painfully in his chest and he couldn't even breathe.

Seeing Eleni and Gabriel ecstatic over their little girl, seeing Nik and Mia offering them advice, he had felt a cold chill pass through him.

As if a ghost had passed through him, his father's ghost. Clearly the pace he had been setting for himself was driving him mad. Finally, he would be like Theos in this, too.

But the laughter he imagined, the mocking *I win* smile that his father would have worn, knowing that he had won in the end—that he had made Andreas as hard and ruthless as him, as he'd always wanted to… it was the thing that broke through his self-imposed punishment.

God, he felt so tired in his heart. So alone and utterly miserable.

He'd tried his hardest to keep away from Ariana, used every tenet he'd used in life to stay strong enough for his father, but nothing worked.

He loved her so much. He missed her so much. Even when she'd hated him, his life had felt more alive than like this. Being near her, sleeping wrapped up around her, smelling the scent of her on his sheets—it had been hellish.

Walking away every time was like losing a limb.

A torture treatment designed just for him.

He wanted to protect her. He wanted to give her a chance to walk away. To find life away from him. To find her happiness without him.

But *Thee mou*, the stubborn woman didn't go. She was in his skin, in his blood, in his soul. With her, he felt complete. He felt joy unlike anything he'd ever known.

He had snubbed her, avoided her, stonewalled her for two months, ripping away his own heart in the process. But she was nowhere near gone from his mind or body or soul.

He had tried to live without her. And it was slowly, but surely, unraveling him. Heart pounding in his chest, Andreas walked toward their private suite. His long strides were just not long enough today.

He went through her suite and then returned to his own. The silence screamed over his nerves. There were no staff members, nor her, nor any of her friends.

Determined to find her, he turned. Giannis, her aide, stood at the door, his chin lifted high. "Looking for something, Your Highness?"

Andreas felt his knees buckling under him. Had she left him again? Had he finally driven her away?

Giannis knew. Of course, her little friend knew. And whose fault was that when he wouldn't even give her the time of the day? When he had used her for pleasure but wouldn't even meet her eyes?

Ariana needed so much, deserved so much in life and once again, all he'd done was starve her.

"Where is she?" Panic made getting the words out so hard.

"She left," Giannis said with something like sympathy in his eyes.

Andreas nodded and gritted his teeth. "She left me then."

"No, she...she said she needed a break. That she needed time to think. She...said she would go back to the only place in the world where she'd been happy.

"Delirious with joy," he said, imitating Ariana's fondness for superlatives.

Ariana and he had both been happy, delirious with joy, in only one place.

Only one place where the world had been at bay. Where it had been just them. Made for each other.

Andreas stilled against the door, his heartbeat slowly returning to normal. At least she hadn't run away. She hadn't left him. He extended his hand to the other man, who looked on it with complete disbelief in his eyes. Finally, when he shook his hand, Andreas smiled. "Thank you for always being her friend, Giannis."

Giannis gave him a completely unnecessary bow of his head. "I would give my life for my Queen, Your Highness. She is worth it, even when she had been just a friend who asked about my *ya-ya*."

"She is," Andreas whispered.

New life breathed in his veins. He knew where she was. He would find her and he would tell her how much he loved her. He was a weaver of words, a teller of past tales, a world-class orator.

How could words be hard to come by in the most important thing of his life?

Within minutes, he asked for a chopper. Since no pilot was available in the last minute, Nikandros volunteered to give him a quick "lift." Andreas had a feeling Nik was only coming along to see Andreas suffer.

"Thank God, Andreas. Eleni and Mia were planning another intervention for you, and only Eleni's labor put a stop to that. Gabriel thought we should simply knock you over the head with a club. Repeatedly, until you came to your senses."

A long time ago, Andreas would have been extremely uncomfortable with the conversation. He wouldn't have seen the point in it, even. What point was there in discussing and pouring out one's feelings to a brother or a friend when those feelings had to be suppressed anyway?

He laid his head back against the seat rest and smiled. "I would not have minded that, Nikandros. I would even go so far as to say I probably needed that. But you tell Marquez that and I will deny it."

Laughter boomed in his ears. "Only loyalty to my King forbids me to tell him that, Andreas. Gabriel would love nothing better, believe me.

"You deserve happiness. Did I ever tell you that?"

His eyes flew open, he stared at Nik. "No. But Camille has. A lot of times. Whether I paid attention to her or not, she repeated it again and again. That it was okay for me to feel anger, want, affection, jealousy, even inadequacy. I don't think I ever told you this, Nik, but I thank you for sharing your mother with me. I would not have known any kindness if not for Camille."

His blue eyes glittering, Nikandros looked away. "Among all three of us, you deserve it the most."

"I'm sure Mia would not agree with that."

"I think she would. You walked the hardest path with Theos. You could have become like him. I worried it was already too late for you. I was terrified you would never know the happiness I know with Mia."

"All because of him."

"I almost didn't. But Camille and you and Eleni… and Ariana…" He swallowed the emotion that sat in his throat like a boulder. Gabriel, the smug bastard, had been right. "Ariana saved me." She had done it even then.

He just hadn't been able to see it. Or understand it.

With one smile, and an outrageous question, she had melted the ice around his heart.

She was right. He was ready. He was a different man. A man who could love the extraordinary woman his wife had become.

Soon, they were up in the sky. Andreas clutched the book in his hands, his book. It was the only thing he had to give her, other than his heart, the only thing that would be valuable to her. The only thing she would truly appreciate.

Ariana had spent most of her first day trying to locate the owner of the old log cabin. The sleepy fishing village had no registration office to speak of. So she had just haunted the old café where she had worked.

But before she could ask a single question, she had been recognized. As the King's wife, Ariana Drakos. The Queen. Thankfully also as the girl who had worked there for one summer a long time ago. She had instantly been mobbed by the friendly crowd, for whom her appearance was a once-in-a-lifetime thing.

In the end, she had eaten dinner there, made a reservation at a nearby hotel, but had no more knowledge about the owner.

The second day had gone with more useless searching and then sleeping away the rest of the day because she had been exhausted.

Tears filled her eyes. Damn it, all she wanted was to have a quick look inside. To bolster her faltering faith in Andreas and her.

She dashed away the tears as she dressed on the third morning. She cried over every small thing these days.

Dressed in jeans and a thick sweater, oversized and falling to her knees, she had stolen from Andreas's closet, she pulled on knee-high boots. She thought she was hungry until she stopped at a coffee shop. Instead the smell of it sent her hurrying away from the cute café. She wasn't able to get much dinner into herself, either.

She grabbed a map instead. She knew the trail through the forested woods pretty well, but it had been ten years.

Pulling a knit cap tight on her head so that a bit of her hair was covered too, as she had totally forgotten about being recognized, she made her way past the first sign.

The air was redolent with scents of pine. She slid her hands under her armpits. She had also forgotten how cold it got here during winter, so close to the mountains. Her spirits lifted as she realized she could make out the path without referring to the map at all.

Fifteen minutes later, she was breathing hard—something else she *had* forgotten about was the steep climb at the end—but standing in front of the log cabin.

The red exterior was gleaming as well as it had been back then. The area in front of it was as always neatly cleared. A huge pile of freshly chopped wood sat on one side. Smoke came out of the chimney.

Her eyes filled up again. But she was extremely glad that someone had lived here all these years. Had taken such good care of it.

Now that she was here, she couldn't return without a look inside. Heart beating with a renewed energy, she walked up the small steps to the porch and knocked on the door.

"Kalimera..." She began her practiced speech before the door swung open completely. "I'm so sorry to bother..."

Andreas was standing inside the cabin, his arm on the top side of the door, his eyes devouring her with a tangible hunger.

"Kalimera, Ariana. Will you not come in?"

Stunned, lost for words, Ariana nodded and stepped inside. Suddenly, she didn't at all feel brave. She felt vulnerable and lonely. And juvenile, if the look in Andreas's eyes was anything to go by.

She caught the groan that rose. Why hadn't she realized he would just see it as another ploy for his attention?

Did she really care if he did?

Taking in his long legs and taut behind, clad in tight jeans and the sheer breadth of his masculinity, she also felt deprived. As if the most delicious dessert was placed in front of her but she was not allowed to touch it.

His hair was curling over the collar of his shirt, over which he had worn a thick sweater like her. The scent of sandalwood soap that he used left a thread in the air and she hungrily followed it into the lounge.

Her eyes wide, she looked around the cozy hall. Everything was gleaming and polished. Everything was exactly as they had left it. There was even a reference book of Andreas's and a magazine of hers. Not collecting dust. But neatly arranged.

She frowned. Wait—what was Andreas doing here? So soon after she had left, too?

"You look beautiful," he said in that deep voice behind her and she turned.

Far too fast apparently, because she was suddenly dizzy and would have knocked herself into the pillar if he hadn't caught her.

She shook her head trying to find her balance again while he watched her from under those thick lashes. Scowling. "I don't know what happened." She cleared her throat, and stepped back from his grasp of her hands.

Which didn't go unnoticed.

"I... I just came by to see this place." A lump lodged in her throat as she spotted the shiny silver frame on the mantel. It was still here? She had bought it in a junk shop in this very same village.

She plucked it off the shelf and once again, breath left her. Another picture of her. This one in her wedding dress—or rather the pink, frilly dress that she had worn that morning.

She looked absolutely, utterly in love. And full of happiness.

Hands shaking, she put away the frame and turned. To find him leaning against the pillar, staring at her.

"What are all these things, our things, doing here? I tried to find out who had bought the place but no one really knew. I... I thought it would have become a relic. Like us," she said, and looked away.

She was not going to cry. She was not going to beg.

"I own it," he finally said, and her head whipped up. "I should say, we own it."

"When? When did you buy it?"

"The moment we left here." He looked around at the high ceilings just like she had done. Rubbed the smoothly polished wood with affection. "It took a while to convince the old guy who lived here...but finally he caved."

"Of course—the Crown Prince want something and not get it?"

In two quick strides, he reached her, crowding her along the wall. "What is that supposed to mean?"

She licked her lips, suddenly nervous. She had never seen him like this, so blatantly aggressive. "I... It's not like you're used to being denied what you want, Andreas."

He frowned. "True, but I never used the weight of the crown to persuade this guy. I just told him it was the place where I spent a week trapped with my future wife, the one woman I was going to spend my life with, and that persuaded him.

"It turned out he was an utter romantic."

She nodded, working hard to keep her gaze on his face when the column of his throat beckoned. "You never told me."

A sigh fell from his lips. "I meant for it to be a surprise. I thought we could come back here regularly, but..."

"But everything fell apart when we returned to the city," she finished. God, she had had enough of these games. "Well, I'm sure it would have been a nice gesture." She slipped away from his grasp and faced him. "It works out for me, at least."

"What works out for you?"

"I... I'm not returning to the Palace with you, assuming that's why you're here, *ne*?"

"For what?"

"Stop answering questions with questions."

He put up his hands, as if she was the one being unreasonable. She was totally not prepared for dealing with him here. Any more of this and she'd dissolve into a puddle of tears. "You're here because you think I'm throwing one of my fits and you need to chase me back to the palace for some weighty matter that requires your wife.

"There's four days before the next state dinner and I'll be by your side that morning."

He shrugged. "*Kala.* I will inform Petra we will both return that morning."

"You're crazy. There must be a hundred details to see to."

"As you've pointed out in the past, I have three teams to do my bidding and to arrange my life and one of them will see to the hundred details. I was going to write the speech myself anyway and I can focus better here."

Tears filled her eyes. "Why are you playing with me, Andreas? What is it you want of me?" Her heart felt like it was shattering anew.

He pulled her into his arms instantly. "I didn't mean to make you cry. *Thee mou*, do not cry, *agapita*. I just... You looked so beautiful, so painfully lovely standing there that I forgot what I meant to say.

"I have not come to take you back. In fact, to hell with the dinner if you just want to hole up here for a couple of months. I have enough wood and food to see us through the winter." Now Ariana was alternately laughing and crying into his sweater.

"Why are you here?"

"I...came to give you something." He plucked a book, his book, from the coffee table and handed it to her.

Smiling, Ariana opened the jacket, read the dedication. Again. "I saw it in your bedroom months ago. I... I've been even reading it when you're..." She looked up and flushed. "When you're not there.

"It made me feel like you were still there with me. Especially, the part of you that I fell in love with."

He nodded and swallowed. "Ariana, will you ever forgive me?"

Words did not come, choked by the tears. She shook her head, then nodded, a deluge of emotions drowning her. "If you forgive me."

His mouth came down on hers. Frantic words fell from his mouth as he kissed her, and tasted her. Ariana didn't know whether she was crying or laughing.

Her heart jumped into her throat when he went to his knees in front of her and looked up at her.

He was so tall that his head still reached her abdomen. She buried her hands in his hair, her heart bursting to full.

"I love you so much. My life is empty of joy, of laughter, of everything without you, *glykia mou*.

"Will you come back to me, Ari? Will you come back because I love you and I can't live without you?"

Ari nodded and fell to her knees. He caught her in his arms and she burst into sobs. Pitiful, wrenching sobs that she could not stop no matter what she did.

Andreas felt as if his heart would shatter all over again. God, he couldn't bear her tears. He couldn't stand the wretched sound of her grief. How heartless he had been to bring her to this?

He pulled her into his lap as he'd done once, a long time ago. Fingers stealing into her hair, he pulled her face up, until she was forced to look at him. "I promised myself I would never again hurt you, Ari. Not at any cost.

"Rage at me. Punch me. But forgive me, *pethi mou*. Forgive me for taking this long to understand this thing between us.

"I adore you. I love you so much that I'm still terrified of all the tumult I feel."

He kissed her mouth and she sighed against him. "I would like to answer one of your questions."

She frowned. "Which one?"

"About why I hadn't publicized that manuscript."

"I know why," she said wiping her eyes. "You didn't want to take away the faith and fantasy it gave the people. I even understand how hard it must have been because it was your life's work, your real passion."

He shook his head. "No. I...think I didn't like it myself. I didn't like that he so easily sacrificed the woman he loved. Even when I didn't understand why, it didn't sit well with me.

"It almost felt like if I revealed it, it would become

true. Almost a sentence, a fate for all the rulers of Drakon.

"Even when I thought you were gone, I needed the happy ending. I needed to believe that I'd had my chance of happiness. That I had grabbed it with both hands while I could.

"But since I learned what price you paid for my—"

It was her turn to shut him up. She did it by kissing him softly, slowly, her entire being soaring with that kiss. By pouring all the love she felt for him into the slide of her mouth. "No, no past, Andreas. Only future."

He nodded and wrapped his arms around her. His big palms came to rest on her tummy and suddenly Ariana knew. The dizziness, the nausea at the smell of coffee when she usually needed an IV of it, the lack of hunger…

She shivered violently and he was instantly in front of her. Concern etched in his face. "Ari? What is it?"

"I'm not sure. But I think…" She pulled his hand to her tummy and held it there. "I think we're pregnant."

The silence, which lasted maybe only ten seconds truthfully, stretched her nerves taut. "I don't know how it happened. It's not something I planned without telling you, I mean—"

With a soft growl that made her laugh, he plucked her off the ground as if she were a featherweight. "No more disappearing without telling anyone. No more eating at strange times. And definitely no more sudden twisting and twirling."

He wasn't even out of breath when he put her on the bed and came on top of her. His lower body flush against hers, he propped himself on his elbow. "Is this okay?" he asked, signaling to his body over hers.

Ariana nodded, determined to hold back the tears. Deep grooves etched around his mouth, a wary concern in his eyes. It was clear that the King of Drakon was absolutely terrified. Thankfully, with him by her side, she was not. She stretched like a cat under him and arched into the arousal she could feel against her leg. "You can do whatever you want to me."

A gleam in his eyes, he kissed her tenderly for a long time. Torturously slow when all Ariana wanted was to feel him inside her.

When he let her come up for air, Ari pushed him back on the bed and laid her head on his chest. She didn't know how long they lay like that, staring at each other, smiling sometimes, nibbling at each other's lips other times. Not needing words.

"Do you want a boy or a girl?" she finally asked.

He placed his palm on her tummy, and lifted his eyes to hers. "I do not care. I just want you both safe. I just... I can't imagine my life if something were to happen to you, Ari."

She kissed his temple, his brows, the tip of his arrogant nose, trying to soothe the raw fear in his voice. "Nothing will happen. Not as long as we're together."

He nodded and swallowed. Looked away. Another silence followed, his fingers tight against hers.

She knew he was processing all this. Knew that the emotion he felt for her, the depth of his love for her... it was not an easy thing for him. So she waited, her heart full of tenderness and love. She would wait an eternity for the privilege of being loved by Andreas.

He looked down at her, a fierce light in his dark eyes. "All I know is that you will be a fierce, wonderful mother and I... This child will be so lucky to have you.

"I am so lucky to have found you, Ariana."

Ariana nodded, and reached for his kiss again. "And I'm honored you chose me, Andreas, of all the countless gorgeous, accomplished, beautiful women that have the hots for you all over the world."

He laughed, and she laughed because she loved his laugh. Covering her body, still smiling, he pulled her sweater off. A devilish gleam in his eyes as he realized the sweater was his.

"You have to stop filching my clothes," he said, with his wicked mouth buried against her neck.

"Never," she replied arching into the sensuous warmth of his body.

"*Kala*. You can have my sweaters, my shirts. And my heart."

She loved him so much that her heart felt like it would never settle down. "And you have mine," she managed to whisper somehow just as he licked the puckered crest of her nipple.

Sinking her hands into his hair, she held him tight.

He was the people's man. He had duties to so many. So many responsibilities. Even his time was not his own.

But his kisses and his laughter had always been hers and only hers.

She didn't need anything more than that.

EPILOGUE

Seven months later

THE KING OF DRAKON jumped out of the chopper mere seconds after it hit the tiled terrace of the King's Palace, heart thundering in his chest.

He was late. Damn it, he'd promised her he'd be by her side and he was late. He'd gone half-crazy being stuck in a cabin on the other side of the world, locked in by a hurricane while she had needed him. Even their communication had been cut off and once her labor had started, Andreas could not distract her just to reassure himself.

At least she was not alone, he consoled himself. Nikandros and Mia, Gabriel and Eleni and even Nik's mother, Camille, had been with her. They would have seen to her every need.

The knowledge that she had delivered and both she and the baby were fine was the only thing that had kept him from going utterly mad.

She and the baby had even been transported back to the palace. When Nik would have spilled the beans to the public, Andreas had forbidden him.

He wanted to see her first. He wanted to see for

himself whether his wife had given him a boy or a girl. He needed, desperately, to be a husband and a father, at least for a few minutes, before he had to think like a King. Before he had to make an announcement that Drakon had its heir.

Without breaking his stride, he handed off his laptop case, his long jacket and gloves to his waiting teams. He checked his phone and let another curse fly.

A day, he was late by a whole day.

Long strides took the stairs three and four at a time and by the time he reached his wife's suite, his heart had crawled up into his throat.

The silence hit him hard, ratcheting up his pulse, forming all kinds of scenarios in his head. Uncaring of the sounds he made, he rushed to the huge bed in the center of the room.

Only when he saw her did his breath return to normal.

She lay in the center of the huge bed, a little pale, dark shadows under her eyes, far too thin in his mind. And absolutely beautiful in that glowing, tired kind of way. He was about to reach for her when he heard the soft cry.

A gurgle to be exact.

Like a man possessed, he followed the sound to the tiny crib sitting in the corner of the room. Breath punched through his throat as he looked at the tall infant staring up at him with jet-black eyes.

Long lashes. A thin blade of a nose. Thick hair the color of a raven's wing.

It was like looking at his own reflection—except pudgy, toothless and utterly adorable.

Another gurgle. Almost a command.

His knees buckling, Andreas had to hold on to the wall beside him. This was a part of him—his own flesh and blood. And the emotion that filled his body threatened to take him out at the knees.

"Pick him up," said a husky voice behind him. "He wants you to pick him up."

Andreas jerked around, tears blurring his vision. "Him?" he whispered, past the lump in his throat. "It's a boy?"

Her own eyes luminous with tears, Ariana nodded. Hauling her into his arms, he pressed a rough kiss to her mouth. The taste of her exploded through his body, an anchor, a siren's call. Home.

He tried to swallow her grief—the memory of the son they'd lost—into him when she trembled. When tears leaked out the corners of her beautiful eyes. "We'll always have his memory," he whispered against her temple and felt her answering shudder.

He crushed her to him, uncaring of how feeble she was. God, he needed the warmth of her body. Needed to hear the hitch of her breath as he peppered kisses all over her face. "Have I told you how much I love you?" he said, his throat gruff and scratchy. "I'm so sorry, *agapita*. I'm sorry I wasn't here when you needed me."

Sinking her fingers into his hair, she brought his face up. "No apologies needed. Not if you promise to be here for the next three."

Laughter burst out of him at the running joke between them. He'd said one, terrified of losing her, and Ariana had said they would have four. Flushed and breathtakingly beautiful, she made it look so easy that for the first time, four seemed like a splendid idea.

"It's a deal," he said against her mouth, wild with

love. Crazy with a soul-deep longing that he knew would never abate.

That he knew was his strength in all things.

A loud growl came again from the crib and Ariana dissolved into giggles against his mouth. "Your son demands your attention, Your Highness."

"Does he?" Andreas asked, stalling for time.

And she knew. Somehow, his wife knew how terrified he was. By how much he wanted to do right by his tiny son. By how much he already loved that little infant. By how inadequate he felt for the task.

Leaning her forehead against his, she met his gaze. "If you love him half as much as you love me, Andreas, he will know it. He will know it and he will love you back just as much," she said with a confidence that unmanned him. Another quick kiss over his lips. A tug in his hair. "Go hold your son, before his numerous cousins descend upon us."

Nodding, Andreas stood up and walked toward the crib. *His son.* It was as if the entire world had tilted on its axis and refused to return to normal.

Hands shaking, he lifted the chubby body that was only as big as his forearm. Heart in his throat, he walked to the bed and climbed into it. His son wailed as Andreas settled him snugly against Ariana, his forehead all scrunched up.

"He's a little high-maintenance, isn't he?" Andreas whispered, awed by the tiny fingers that had latched onto his mother's breast.

"Like someone I know," Ariana said with a glorious smile. A blush climbed up her chest and her neck as Andreas unabashedly watched his son suckle at her breast. He had thought he couldn't be any happier these past months. But now his family was complete.

Theos had had all this with him, Eleni and Nikandros. But he had ruined it all with his own hands.

Andreas would never let that happen to him. His life, his fate had delineated from the moment he had seen Ariana in that café and he was thankful for that moment a million times over.

Sliding down on the bed, he buried his nose in her neck, the ever-present desire a thrum under his skin.

"How long is he going to do that?" he asked, a wicked growl in his voice.

She frowned. "A few months at the least. Why?"

Andreas licked the pulse at her throat, tasted the salt and scent of her. His body's tiredness melted away, his world tilting on its axis again. "I just don't like sharing what's mine. Even with him," he whispered, and laughed when his wife blushed.

She was his Queen, a lawyer with a fierce reputation and now a mother. But when she looked at him like that, she was only the woman he loved with all his heart. The woman who'd made his life worth living.

"I'll always be yours first, Your Highness," she whispered against his mouth, and Andreas fell all over in love again.

* * * * *

If you enjoyed HIS DRAKON RUNAWAY BRIDE
don't forget to read the first two parts of
THE DRAKON ROYALS *trilogy*

CROWNED FOR THE DRAKON LEGACY
THE DRAKON BABY BARGAIN

And also by Tara Pammi...

MARRIED FOR THE SHEIKH'S DUTY
THE SURPRISE CONTI CHILD
THE UNWANTED CONTI BRIDE

All available now!

#3565 UNDONE BY THE BILLIONAIRE DUKE
by Caitlin Crews

Eleanor Andrews refuses to see gorgeous Hugo, Duke of Grovesmoor, as anything but her boss! Hugo might be jaded and cynical, but innocent Eleanor fires his blood—and he can't turn down the challenge to unbutton his uptight employee!

#3566 HIS MAJESTY'S TEMPORARY BRIDE
The Princess Seductions
by Annie West

Cat Dubois's life as an illegitimate royal hasn't been luxurious. But when her princess half sister disappears ahead of her engagement to King Alexander, Cat agrees to step in! She didn't anticipate Alex's electric attraction—and Cat cannot hold back from his caress...

#3567 BOUND BY THE MILLIONAIRE'S RING
The Sauveterre Siblings
by Dani Collins

Millionaire Ramon Sauveterre will do anything to keep the spotlight off his family. Including faking an engagement to his head of PR, Isidora Garcia! She never forgave Ramon for breaking her heart. But resisting Ramon's heated touch proves utterly impossible!

#3568 THE VIRGIN'S SHOCK BABY
One Night With Consequences
by Heidi Rice

Megan never expected her plan to discover Dario De Rossi's business plans would lead to his bed! When Megan is violently punished, he's honor bound to protect her. But Megan has amnesia, believes they're in love...and she's carrying his baby!

YOU CAN FIND MORE INFORMATION ON UPCOMING HARLEQUIN® TITLES, FREE EXCERPTS AND MORE AT WWW.HARLEQUIN.COM.

HPCNM0917RB

Charlotte hadn't touched a man since Rafe. She'd had no
interest.

She needed to find some interest. Because she was going
to have a normal life. Whatever she did, it would be her
choice. And that was the point.

She didn't know what answers she had expected to find
here. Right now, the only clear answer seemed to be that her
body, her heart, was still affected by him.

He excused himself from the group, and suddenly he was
walking her way. And she froze. Like a deer caught in the
headlights. Or rather, like a woman staring at Rafe Costa.

She certainly wasn't the only woman staring. He moved
with fluid grace, and if she didn't know better, she would
never have known his sight was impaired at all.

He was coming closer, and as he did her heart tripped over itself, her hands beginning to shake. She wished she could touch him.

Oh, she wanted it more than anything. In that moment, she wanted it more than her next breath. To put her hands on Rafe Costa's face one more time. To kiss those lips again. To place her hand over his chest and see if she could still make his heart race.

It was easy to forget that her stepmother had told her how Rafe had left, taking an incentive offered by her father to end his tenure there earlier. It was easy to forget that and remember instead the way it had felt when he had kissed her. Touched her. The way she had pleaded with him to take her virginity, to make her his in every way.

Really, he had never wanted her. He had simply been toying with her.

She should remember that. Her treacherous, traitorous body should remember that well. But it didn't. Instead it was fluttering. As if a host butterflies had been set loose inside her.

Suddenly, he was there. So close that if she wanted to she could reach out and touch the edge of his sleeve with her fingertips.

Could bump into him accidentally, just to make contact. He wouldn't know it was her. He couldn't.

Suddenly, he turned. He was looking past her, his dark eyes unseeing, unfocused. But then he reached out and unerringly grabbed hold of her wrist, dragging her toward his muscular body.

"Charlotte."

HPEXP092017

Coming next month—*Bound by the Millionaire's Ring*, the third part of Dani Collins's The Sauveterre Siblings quartet! Angelique, Henri, Ramon and Trella make up the world's most renowned family—wherever they go, scandal is sure to follow. They're protected by the best security money can buy, but what happens when each of these Sauveterre siblings meets the one person who can breach their heart?

The Sauveterre playboy is about to acquire a temporary fiancée…

Millionaire race-car driver Ramon Sauveterre is no stranger to fame, but he'll do just about anything to keep the spotlight off his family. Including faking an engagement to his gorgeous head of PR, Isidora Garcia!

Isidora cannot forgive Ramon for dragging her into this farce— just as she'll never forgive him for the indiscretion that broke her heart. But while their relationship might be a deception, the burning longing his kisses spark is all too real—and resisting Ramon's heated touch until the end of their arrangement proves utterly impossible!

Bound by the Millionaire's Ring
Available October 2017!

Pursued by the Desert Prince
His Mistress with Two Secrets
Available now!

And don't miss the final part—Trella and Xavier's story— available January 2018!

LOVE
Harlequin
romance?

Join our Harlequin community to share your thoughts and connect with other romance readers!

Be the first to find out about promotions, news, and exclusive content!

Sign up for the Harlequin e-newsletter and download a free book from any series at

www.TryHarlequin.com
